RAVE

The Better to Kiss You With

"4 ½ stars… It was so well written that I never once doubted it. The last part of the book was very exciting and full of threat and suspense."

—*Inked Rainbow Reads Reviews*

"4 ½ stars… I really enjoyed the writing style of Ms. Osgood and hope to read more by her in the future. Her voice was so clear and the emotions she brings forth are so rich. I kind of don't want this book to end."

—*Molly Lolly Book Reviews*

"*The Better to Kiss You With* is a heady paranormal romance with a Canadian Gothic atmosphere. Cherry blossoms bloom in a moody, misty spring while terrible notes turn up and computers can haunt more than any presence."

—*Friend of Dorothy Wilde Book Blog*

Huntsmen

Michelle Osgood

interlude 🧩 **press** • new york

interlude press • new york

To Leita.

"You only find yourself when you disobey.
Disobedience is the beginning of responsibility, I think."

—*Guillermo del Toro*

Chapter One |

KIARA'S THUMB TAPPED AGAINST THE wood of the bar to the thrumming pulse of the music. The air in the club was thick with it, and it pressed against her damp skin offering no escape from the heat of dancing bodies packed together. She longed to step outside into the wet February night, but she'd promised Deanna another drink, and despite her physical discomfort she couldn't deny the thrill of the swinging lights and energy of the crowd.

"Oh, my god, I just *love* your necklace!"

She cut her gaze away from the bartender to the boy who'd squeezed in beside her. He reached for her throat, and for a split second a different sort of pulse raced through Kiara's veins.

"Gold isn't really, like, *in* right now, but, girl, you are. Pulling. That. Off."

Kiara bared her teeth. "I know."

His fingers quickly withdrew from the chunky costume jewelry that rested over the slight swell of her breasts. "You look totally fab, though. Like, super fierce."

The bartender moved closer, and Kiara pushed up on her toes so she could lean farther over the bar and try to catch his eye.

"I mean, you're tiny—god, I wish *I* was that tiny—but you've got this total badass aura. Even in that dress you look like you could totally kick my ass."

"Don't tempt me."

He laughed. "Girl you are vicious! You here for the drag show? It's so cute seeing all you ladies with your mascara moustaches and—ow!"

"Oops." Kiara tucked one heavy-toed boot behind the other.

Eyebrows raised in an unspoken question, the bartender finally stepped in front of her.

"Two tequila and sodas. With lime."

"Sodas?" Apparently forgiving Kiara's "accidental" kick, the boy slung his arm around her shoulders. The sweat of his armpit was wet against her bare skin. "Don't be a pussy! Do a shot with me! Two shots of tequila," he informed the bartender.

"I don't want—" But the bartender had placed her drinks in front of her and was pouring the shots.

"Yaaas, queen! Wait, where's the salt?"

The bartender barely blinked. "This is a bar, not a restaurant. That's twelve dollars."

The boy pulled his arm off her and reached for his wallet. Kiara grabbed one shot, tossed it back, and did the same with the second. Not batting an eye, she plucked the two drink glasses off the bar. "He'll buy the drinks."

"Hey, wait. I didn't—" The boy's indignation was swallowed up by the noise of the club as Kiara slipped easily into the crowd. The multi-level club in Vancouver's Gastown neighborhood was packed. Though it wasn't strictly a gay bar—they'd have had to go to Davie Street for that—the club hosted a drag king night once a month. The crowd was primarily queer women and non-binary folk more at ease in the slightly grungy Gastown bar than the glossy dance clubs of Davie.

Working her way through the crowd, Kiara headed for the stairs to the basement level. Bodies closed around her like a wall, but Jamie and Deanna weren't hard to spot. Kiara's cousin and packmate Jamie stood half a head above the crowd, with one muscled arm slung around her girlfriend, who was chubby and radiant in her deep pink dress and blonde curls. Kiara slid in beside them, waving her bounty.

"Thanks, K!" Deanna beamed and pressed the cool side of the plastic glass against her round cheek. She closed her eyes in a moment of bliss. "I can't believe how hot it is in here!"

"I can." The bottle of beer she nursed hung precariously from Jamie's fingertips, and at her temples her hair was damp with sweat. "How long till the show starts?"

Kiara took a sip from her drink as she pulled her phone from her clutch to check the time. "Ten minutes." The brief buzz she'd felt from the shots was fading, and the watered-down tequila in her glass wasn't enough to be a blip on her radar. She was a werewolf; it wasn't that she could *never* get drunk, it was just that it took a significant amount of alcohol to reach a buzz, let alone stay there. She found the effort was rarely worth the reward or the hit to her bank account. As someone jostled past her, causing soda to slosh over the rim of her glass and down her wrist, Kiara reconsidered the idea.

The crowd on the bottom floor was slowly increasing; the press of bodies grew ever tighter as they pushed toward the raised stage at the back of the room.

The night out had been Deanna's idea. Of course. Deanna had insisted that Kings of Hearts was an event not to be missed. "Especially because you're so new to Vancouver," she'd cajoled, green eyes bright and wide and earnest. "Don't you want to meet other queer women?"

"No," had been Kiara's blunt response. And yet here she was.

It wasn't that Kiara didn't like dancing, because she did. She even enjoyed the lights and the pounding music. What she didn't like was the people.

Someone bumped into her again, and Kiara whipped her head around to glare at the girl trying to wriggle past them.

"Sorry." Completely unperturbed by Kiara's scowl, the girl tucked a strand of violet hair behind her ear and gave Kiara a flirty grin.

"Come watch the show with me?" Her touch was light against Kiara's upper arm.

"I'm good. Thanks," Kiara added after Jamie jabbed her elbow into Kiara's side. "What?" she asked Jamie once the girl had vanished into the bodies in front of them. "I was nice."

Jamie arched her eyebrows as she raised her beer to her lips.

"Come on, you two. This is fun!" Beside them, Deanna practically vibrated with excitement. It was almost infectious. Almost.

"I checked on Facebook, and Terence Stallion is here tonight!" At Jamie and Kiara's blank looks, Deanna sighed. "She—or *he*, rather—is supposed to put on a great show. Nathan saw him once and mooned about the performance for a month."

"Nathan would moon about anyone for a month," Kiara responded.

"True," Deanna conceded.

Despite Kiara's best efforts, they were slowly being pushed toward the stage as more and more people spilled down the stairs. A bead of sweat ran down Kiara's nape, and she copied Deanna's earlier idea, pressing the cold plastic of her icy drink against her breastbone. The resulting chill was brief, but welcome.

Just as Kiara was wondering if she could elbow her way out of the crowd and grab them more drinks—not for the alcohol, but for the ice—the lights in the bar winked out. Kiara barely blinked, but her feet planted themselves more firmly against the sticky club floor, readied for a fight. A couple girls shrieked: an utterly feminine combination of fear and excitement and anticipation. Deanna, naturally, was one of them. The sound was reassuring, and, as a bright white light swept over the room before illuminating the stage, Kiara allowed herself to relax. Maybe she did need to get out more.

"Ladies! Welcome to Kings of Hearts!" the host shouted over the sound system, and was answered by an explosion of screams from the crowd. "We've got an excellent show for you tonight. Are you ready?"

Deanna laughed and grabbed Jamie's hand, twining their fingers together. *What the hell*, Kiara thought, and raised her hand to her lips to join in the cacophony with an ear-splitting wolf whistle. It was worth it to see Jamie wince and Deanna grin happily at her.

"That's what I like to hear! Our first performance is a duo that knows *exactly* how to make you scream." On stage the emcee, an older butch woman, waggled her eyebrows behind her glasses. "So hang on to your panties—those of you wearing them—and welcome to the stage Phil Anders and Roland in the Deep!"

Two kings, one Black and the other white, both impeccably dressed, strutted onto the stage as the opening bars of their song spilled through the club. One swung an elegant cane, and the other adjusted the hang of his pocket watch against his three-piece suit. Cheers erupted as the two dropped into a choreographed routine about being a classic, street-elegant old-fashioned man.

Kiara, enjoying the show as the two performers spun and flashed, let her head nod in time to the music. The lights glinted over their skins and illuminated the painstakingly applied facial hair. Around her, the press of people became stifling. More patrons crowded into the smaller basement as word of the show trickled up to the main room. Yet the scent of joy—mingled as it was with sweat, booze, and a hundred different perfumes—that pervaded the space caused Kiara to shelve her irritation, even as more soda spilled from her cup and ran down her wrist. No matter how grumpy masses of humanity made her, Kiara wasn't monster enough to vilify a club full of LGBTQ+ folks who had created a space in which they were happy and carefree.

Who knows, she mused as the pair onstage wrapped up their performance, she might have a good night after all.

"You want another drink?" Jamie had to bend close to Kiara's ear and shout over the between-acts song. Kiara glanced at her glass; she was nearly finished, with less than a mouthful—ice and all—left. She nodded. She tossed back the rest of her drink and passed her glass to Jamie as Deanna did the same.

"Thanks, babe!" Deanna called, leaning up to give Jamie a peck on the cheek. Despite the dim lighting, Kiara had no trouble seeing the blush rise to Jamie's cheeks. Kiara rolled her eyes. Anyone would think the pair of them were just starting to date, never mind going on their tenth month of living together.

The emcee bounded back onstage. "Hot damn! Those are my kind of classic men! And if you've had enough of elegant gentlemen… if you're maybe in the mood for something a little… dirtier—" She gave a roguish wink. "We've got Terence Stallion—" She paused to let the screaming die down; when it became obvious that the crowd had no intention of shutting up, the emcee made a show of throwing up her hands in exasperation before she walked off the stage with a dismissive wave.

The pulsing interlude faded out, and new music came on.

"This is the one Nathan loves!" Deanna looped her arm through Kiara's and gave an excited wriggle as the next performer's song rose. It was "Wilderness" by Nick Jonas—one of Kiara's secret, guilty pleasures. With Deanna's infectious enthusiasm beside her, Kiara couldn't resist her own anticipatory grin as the performer swaggered onto the stage.

Whereas the previous two performers had been faultlessly put together, this king swaggered onto the stage with a thorough air of debauchery. His jacket was held carelessly over one shoulder; the gray tie was so loose around his long neck that it was a mere suggestion of decorum. The buttons on his white shirt were undone to expose a line of golden skin, and long, dark hair spilled from under the cocky jaunt of his hat. In the spinning lights Kiara could just make out the light dusting of carefully applied facial hair, barely enough to sketch the sharp outline of his jaw. As the first lines of the song began, the king tossed his hat into the surging crowd of eager women and held up a defiant face.

His dark eyes locked directly onto hers, and the world fell from beneath Kiara.

Ryn.

Chapter Two |

SHOCK NUMBED KIARA AND HELD her frozen on the dance floor. On stage, Ryn hadn't missed a beat of her routine. With Nick Jonas's voice urging the audience to take themselves back to the wilderness, back to the discovery of desire, and Taryn's long, lean body suggesting all the things that might entail, flashes of memory slammed into Kiara like fists:

Ryn's hands clenched in Kiara's hair, the hard press of parted, demanding lips against her own;

Kiara arched over Ryn, her sightless gaze on the water-damaged ceiling of Ryn's apartment as pleasure shuddered through her;

Running through the woods with the snow cold under clawed feet. Their mouths hung open and panting as their breath steamed in the crisp air.

The slick taste of Ryn in her mouth, the tangle of their limbs.

Now that she was aware of Ryn's presence, Ryn's scent overwhelmed everything else. She smelled the same, like skin-warmed leather, heated by accents of orange peel and cloves, overlaid by the eyelash glue under Ryn's ghost of a beard and her not-quite-scentless deodorant, smelled as strong as though Ryn's arms were around her.

"Oh, man." Deanna's voice was low and reverent, possibly not meant for Kiara's ears under the music and the noise. She fanned herself with her free hand. "Nathan wasn't exaggerating."

"We need to leave." The words stuck in Kiara's throat. She wasn't sure if she'd said them aloud.

"What?" Deanna asked, not pulling her eyes from the stage. "No, we don't."

"Yes." Kiara yanked her arm free from Deanna; panic sharpened her voice. "We need to go."

Deanna turned to her; the lights made the worry stark on her face. "What's going on?" She reached out, but Kiara jerked back, uncharacteristically graceless, and knocking into the person behind her.

"Watch it," the younger woman chided.

"Sorry," Kiara said.

"Seriously, why—"

"Leaving. Now."

"Good." Jamie was suddenly at Kiara's shoulder and was strung so tight with tension she echoed Kiara. "You saw them, too."

Kiara's gaze moved to the stage and Ryn's continued performance. It took everything she had to pull her attention back and focus on her cousin. Anxiety rolled off Jamie; the sharp spike of it made a jagged counterpoint to the thick roll of lust that permeated the air of the club.

"How did you—" Jamie hadn't met Ryn. None of them had. They'd known about her, sure, but Ryn had been Kiara's, just Kiara's. How could Jamie recognize someone she'd never seen?

"An axe." Jamie continued as though she hadn't heard Kiara. Her chest heaved. "At first I thought, coincidence. But then, another. That can't be—" She broke off, and her eyes left Kiara to dart around at the strangers surrounding them.

"Axes?" Deanna's green eyes widened. "There are people here with axes?" Her voice rose, terror closer at hand in queer spaces since Orlando.

Trying to shut out the sound of the crowd, of the music, Kiara pressed her fingers to her temples.

From the way Jamie was talking, the weight she'd given the word "axe," Jamie could only mean one thing—as impossible as it sounded. Huntsmen.

The crowd seemed to press closer; the mass of people, which had been simply irritating, was now ominous. The Huntsmen were human. Nothing distinguished them from regular club patrons, save for the way they marked themselves: with the symbol of an axe.

Fear clawed Kiara's throat as she forced herself to look past the crowd and find the club's exits. There were two downstairs, one close to the stage and another across the floor. To wade through the crowd would put them too much at risk. The best option was to go up the stairs and out the front—the narrow stairway meant they couldn't be surrounded, and once they'd reached the top there was only a few feet of open space before the narrow hallway to the club entrance. It was still a risk, but a smaller one.

"Okay. You two have to leave. Now." Kiara grabbed Deanna's arm in one hand and Jamie's in the other, steering them with inhuman strength to the back of the room.

"You're not coming?" Jamie held tight to Deanna's hand, as her partner frowned in confusion.

"I'll follow." The lights spun from the stage and illuminated the crowd around them. Hands were waved high, and people were cheering as the song reached its climax.

Three people away, one of those raised hands led to a forearm with an unmistakable tattoo: an axe's thick black lines stark against the woman's pale skin.

"Go. Now." Kiara shoved Jamie and Deanna through the crowd.

"Why aren't you—"

"I don't understand—"

Kiara cut them off and spoke directly to Jamie. "It's Taryn. Onstage. Ryn."

Jamie closed her eyes in a split second of understanding, then tightened her grip on Deanna and tugged her toward the stairs. She'd never met Kiara's first girlfriend, but she'd definitely heard about her. "Come on, Dee, I'll explain when we're outside."

Kiara shoved the shock of seeing Ryn to the back of her mind and ruthlessly slammed the door on any speculation about what and why and how. That didn't matter. Nothing mattered now except getting through the mass of people to the stage, getting Ryn, and getting the two of them out of the bar.

She dropped her glass carelessly, and it rolled against the foot of the girl beside her, who squawked. Kiara was already moving past her. Kiara was small—*tiny*, the boy at the bar had described her—and she used that, sliding through the press of bodies with barely a ripple.

She'd lost the axe wearer in the crowd, but her skin crawled with the knowledge that they were here. Hyperawareness coalesced behind her eyes, like the not-quite-painful pressure of an itch she couldn't scratch.

The last line of the song pumping through the sound system faded out, low and suggestive. On stage, Taryn-as-Terence gave a mocking bow; the jut of her chin told the crowd that she knew it was all a performance, that she had given them exactly what they'd asked for and had risked nothing to do it. The self-assuredness was breathtaking.

Kiara pushed her way to the front of the stage. Ryn rose from her bow. Her dark eyes swept over the upturned, adoring faces before snapping to a stop on Kiara's.

"Huntsmen." Kiara spoke the word conversationally, not bothering to raise her voice over the cacophony of the cheers and the music.

Ryn's nostrils flared, and her eyes widened a fraction before they skipped past Kiara and out to the crowd.

"We have to go."

Ryn jerked her chin down in a barely perceptible nod. Her eyes flicked to the right, and Kiara understood.

Terence blew a smirking kiss to the crowd and sauntered offstage. Kiara wriggled urgently through his swooning fans.

"You can't come back here."

Confronted by an upheld palm, Kiara halted at the stairs that led backstage.

"This area is for performers only." The Latina woman's face was set in bored lines; her yellow shirt identified her as one of the club's staff. Clearly it was not the first time she'd turned someone away that night.

"Look, I'm meeting—"

"Hun, I don't care if you're meeting Evan Rachel Wood herself. Performers only." The woman enunciated the last part without managing to pull her attention from the room behind Kiara.

The prickling behind Kiara's eyes mounted and was echoed in the flesh of her gums.

"Maria, hey." Ryn pushed back the black curtain. "Come on, let her through."

"Tar—" Reluctance was heavy in the woman's voice. "You know I'm not supposed to."

"I won't tell if you won't, 'kay? This is my girlfriend. We won't cause any trouble. Promise." Ryn held out her hand past Maria.

Kiara placed her hand in Ryn's and plastered a smile across her face. "I'll be good." She added a flutter of her eyelashes and coaxed a blush to her cheeks. Ryn's skin was hot under her palm. Touching Ryn had always felt like touching the sun.

"You'd better be," Maria warned as she stepped aside and let Kiara through.

"Thank you." Ryn winked at Maria, and Kiara heard the woman's heartbeat accelerate in response. With a valiant effort, Kiara swallowed her huff of annoyance.

The area backstage was dimly lit. Ryn kept Kiara's hand in hers as she led the way, deftly avoiding the few other performers who loitered about, waiting for their turns onstage.

"We have to go," Kiara repeated. She spoke more loudly now that they were away from everyone else.

"I heard you the first time."

"Then what are we doing?" Kiara's fingers curled perfectly around Ryn's. She wanted to yank her hand free. She wanted to kiss the spot where they fit so well together.

"I have to get my bag."

Ten years. Surely ten years was long enough for feelings to fade, for the memory of what they had been to dull. She shouldn't feel the bright hurt, the greedy hunger, as though it had been yesterday.

In the back of her head a siren screamed, a warning that she didn't have time for this. Kiara's grip on Ryn's hand tightened involuntarily.

"Leave it."

"I'm not leaving it. There's five thousand dollars' worth of equipment in there."

"Ryn, you heard me. The Huntsmen are here."

"Maybe." They reached a set of lockers, and Ryn wriggled her fingers free of Kiara's. "Aren't you the one who told me they're a myth? Do you really think they'd show up in Vancouver? At a *drag king* show?" But even as she spoke she opened the locker door and pulled free a large duffel bag.

"Werewolves are supposed to be myths, too."

"And yet," Ryn conceded. She slung the bag over her shoulder. "My bike is out front."

Kiara shook her head. "We're not going back out there." She had no idea how many Huntsmen were in the crowd. "There's a back exit, a fire door, right?"

"I'm not leaving without my bike." Ryn stared Kiara down.

There was no use arguing. There never was.

"Fine. We'll go around and grab it on our way out. But we have to go." The siren wailed louder. Kiara grabbed Ryn's arm and pushed her toward the back. Ryn snapped her teeth at Kiara and twisted free, but led the way.

As they pushed through the heavy metal door to the alley, Kiara spared a moment to curse under her breath. Cold, insistent rain was coming down, and her coat was inside with the chipper coat-check girl who'd tried to slip Jamie her number as they'd come in.

Now it was Ryn's turn to tug Kiara out from the slight protection of the building. "Is it just you?" she asked as they made their way around the side of the building. Kiara squinted against the rain as Ryn moved through it unconcerned.

"No. Jamie's here and her partner. They'll meet us out front."

As they rounded the corner, Jamie spotted them and hurried over with Deanna in tow. Jamie's lips were pressed together in a worried line. With her wet hair plastered on her head, Deanna looked miserable.

"We have to go," Jamie hissed. "There's one..." She jerked her head at the club door, and the woman with the forearm tattoo stepped through. Outside now, in the glow of the streetlights, Kiara could see her more clearly. The woman's hair was long and straight, an unnatural shade of dark red—*like dried blood*, Kiara thought. Her face was dominated by a pair of strong eyebrows, dyed to match her hair, and her eyes glittered fiercely underneath.

"Come on." Kiara moved down the street with Deanna and Jamie close on her heels. "*Taryn.*"

"I need my bike; hang on." Ryn stood beside an ancient-looking bike chained to a bike rack. The seat was covered with a plastic bag, though in this downpour Kiara doubted it had done any good.

"We don't have time!"

"Excuse me." The woman at the door moved forward and slid her arms through a jacket.

Ryn swore viciously and abandoned the bike. "Let's go, let's go."

They ducked down another alley, and Kiara urged Jamie and Deanna ahead of her so that she could keep an eye out behind them.

It's not really the Huntsmen, Kiara told herself, *they're not* real. Ryn was right; as far as Kiara and her pack were concerned, the Huntsmen were a legend. A group of humans dedicated to hunting dangerous werewolves? It seemed unlikely that an organization like that could operate without the General North American Assembly of Werewolves being aware of it, and Kiara was certain that GNAAW wouldn't allow humans to interfere within their jurisdiction.

Well, she'd been certain until now.

The woman's footsteps rang on the cobblestones behind them, and the three werewolves automatically picked up their pace. Jamie hurried Deanna along with them.

Ryn fell into step beside Kiara. "We'll take a right out to the street. There'll be people there."

Kiara gave a short nod. Jamie was already beginning to veer in that direction. This late on a Friday Gastown was always a hub of nightlife activity, and not even the pouring rain could dampen that. Once they got to the street, they could lose themselves in the roaming packs of drunken, rowdy clubgoers. If this woman was a Huntsman—a Huntress?—she'd be human, and there'd be no way for her to track the werewolves' scent the way another wolf could.

They turned to head down the alley toward the street. The rain wasn't heavy, but it was steady enough that Deanna had her arms wrapped closely around her, and it occurred to Kiara that, like her, Deanna and Jamie had left their coats inside. It didn't matter, though. They could come back tomorrow for them, if they had to. If the Huntsmen were *really*—

Stop, she ordered herself. There was no sense in questioning what both she and Jamie had seen. Better safe than sorry.

Someone stepped into the alley in front of them.

Chapter Three |

KIARA'S LIPS CURLED BACK FROM her teeth in an echo of the growl that rumbled heavily in her throat. Jamie had moved in front of Deanna, who, smart enough to know she'd be no help in a physical altercation, had slid toward the wall. Ryn lowered her bag from her shoulder and kicked it to the side.

The man at the end of the alley, who had the collar on his long coat flipped up against the rain, moved toward them. He was tall with wide shoulders, and his smooth footsteps pointed to training that was probably not received as a civilian. He held his gloved hand up in a demonstration of harmlessness.

"Just give me a minute, girls. I only want to talk."

Ryn snorted. "Not likely," she said under her breath. Kiara agreed.

"There's no need to be defensive."

The man continued toward them. He had a suspicious bulge in his jacket coat and smelled of anticipatory excitement. Kiara glanced over to see Deanna's pale face and wide, scared eyes.

"Agree to disagree." Kiara balanced on the balls of her feet. Her body hummed with tension, and the itch was back in her gums and the tips of her fingers.

Footsteps came from behind them, and Jamie turned. "Two more," she informed them. Jamie lowered into a crouch, and Kiara didn't need to look to know that Jamie's eyes probably weren't their soft brown anymore.

"Let us go, and we won't hurt you." Kiara spoke to the man in front of her. "Turn around, walk away, and this ends."

He shook his head and smiled. "See, that's the problem with lycans. Always threatening violence."

"You started it," Ryn pointed out. She rolled her shoulders and flashed him a grin that was all teeth. "I'm happy to finish it, though."

"Heads up." Jamie's voice was a low warning. "One of them has a gun."

Kiara wasn't going to wait around to see if they were going to use it. She glanced back. The woman from the club and another man advanced. He was smaller than the first, but sturdy and compact with mass that was more muscle than fat. The gun in his hand gleamed in the orange light that filtered into the alley.

"I've got this asshole." Ryn stepped forward, eagerness rolling off her in waves.

"Take the woman. I'll take the gun." No sooner were the words out of Kiara's mouth than the alley exploded with movement. Jamie raced toward the woman, who was reaching into her jacket, and Kiara went for the raised gun.

The man was fast, but not werewolf fast, and the silencer on the barrel lengthened the gun so that Kiara had no trouble sweeping it out of her way. He threw a punch with his other hand. Kiara ducked and rammed her fist into his stomach, which forced the breath out of him in a sudden whoosh. He dropped to the ground. His gun clattered from his fingers. Kiara kicked it away. She could see the tattoo on his neck peeking out over his collar: a black axe that matched the one the woman wore.

Kiara saw Jamie snarling with fury and held at bay at the end of a cattle prod. Ryn had her man on his knees with his arm twisted behind his back and her fingers at his throat. Ryn's knuckles were bloody, and blood ran from his nose.

"You're dangerous." The woman spoke calmly, apparently at ease in the face of three furious werewolves. The prod in front of her crackled.

"We were *dancing*," Jamie spat.

"Drop the weapon, and we'll walk away." Kiara shoved a handful of wet hair from her face. The rain came down harder. She moved closer. "We don't want this."

The man on his knees laughed.

She ignored him. "We don't want to hurt you."

"But you will. You have. And it feels good, doesn't it?" The woman spoke just to Kiara now and she had a gleam in her eyes. "The blood rush, the high, the hunt. You can't help it."

At least on one point, the woman wasn't wrong. Power surged through Kiara's body; her blood thrummed with it. The excited beat of her heart, of Jamie's, of Ryn's, pounded in her ears. Adrenaline sharpened her focus and opened all her senses so that the night was suddenly alive around her. An eager press of wildness ached for release.

"Just because something feels good doesn't mean you have to do it." Kiara took a deep breath. The rain-heavy air was a soothing counterpoint to her heated flesh. She eased the anger, the outrage, and felt the answering tingle along her body as the near-shift melted away. More in control, she held out her hand to the Huntress. "Give it up."

At a sudden movement to her right, Kiara whirled to see the man she'd taken down lunge for the gun. Unprepared, Kiara didn't move fast enough, and then he was on his knees with the barrel pointed, not at her nor Ryn nor Jamie, but steadily at Deanna.

Deanna made a choked-off noise and pressed farther back against the brick wall.

Kiara's control vanished.

She surged forward in a blur of motion. Her hands wrapped around his outstretched arm, and, with a vicious shriek of rage, she hurled him against the brick wall. He hit with a sickening crunch; the gun fell from senseless fingers. Before he'd crumpled to the ground, Kiara whirled to face the other two Huntsmen. Her honey-brown eyes were now ice-gray; when she opened her mouth to speak all that came out was an inhuman snarl.

The woman smirked. "You see? The lycanthropy controls you. You pretend to be normal. You pretend to be people. But you're not."

Kiara lunged for her. Jamie intercepted, her hands digging into Kiara's arms with bruising force as she held her cousin back. The woman laughed and backed away.

Ryn released the man she held and shoved him toward the street. "Run."

He scrambled to his feet.

"Kiara, Kiara, calm down." Jamie refused to let go as the two Huntsmen vanished around the corner. Kiara could *make* her let go. Claws pushed through the tips of her fingers, her toes.

Ryn shouldered Jamie, who instantly moved to Deanna's side.

Unlike Jamie, Ryn kept her hands off of Kiara, but her mere presence barely a foot away blocked any movement Kiara might make. "Control yourself, Kiara," Ryn snapped, with none of Jamie's understanding. "Control yourself."

The too-familiar words jabbed through Kiara's rage. She took a sharp breath and then another. Stepping back from Ryn, she spun around, faced the far wall, and closed her eyes.

Focus, focus, focus. The rain was sharply cold on her shoulders, her bare arms. The pavement was flat and solid under her feet. She smelled sweat, blood, fear. And urine—a constant in downtown alleys. The exercise grounded her, and the urge to shift receded.

Chapter Four |

KIARA TURNED BACK TO THE group. The stormy gray of her eyes gave way to their usual shade of honey gold. Deanna crouched beside the fallen man. Her brow furrowed as she checked his pulse.

"Leave him," Kiara said.

Deanna stared up at her with her eyes wide. Kiara stepped past Jamie and gave Deanna's arm an impatient tug, pulling her to her feet.

"We should call someone though, right? He needs help. He needs an ambulance," Deanna said.

"He pointed a gun at you." Ryn put herself between Deanna and the man's fallen body to block her view.

Kiara kept her senses flung open and did her best to filter through the influx of sensory information to hear if anyone was approaching the alley. "We have to move. There might be more of them."

"Dee, it's okay," Jamie coaxed, wrapping her arm around Deanna's shoulders and hurrying her forward. Deanna's right hand was still balled in a fist. The metal of her keys poked out between her knuckles the way she'd been taught in a half-remembered self-defense class.

"He's human, though. He's a person," Deanna insisted as they hurried from the alley. "He won't heal."

"He'll be fine. They'll come back for him." Ryn's tone indicated that she wasn't thrilled with the thought. "We should be long gone before they do. So where are we going?" She arched an eyebrow as Kiara darted into the street to flag down a cab.

"I know a place. They won't think to look for us there." Kiara hoped so, anyway.

"Who were they after?" Jamie held open the door of the cab that had pulled up to the curb, a van, and helped Deanna in. "How did they know we'd be there?"

"Quiet," Kiara ordered as she gestured for Ryn to get in. "We'll talk about it later." After scrambling in behind Ryn, Kiara slammed the door shut and gave the address to the driver.

As they pulled away, Kiara splayed her hands on her thighs and forced herself to relax them. She had been dangerously close to losing control. As it was, she had shown too much strength—she shouldn't have thrown the Huntsman against the wall, not as hard as she had. Despite Ryn and Jamie's assurances, Kiara wasn't convinced that he'd be "okay." She'd heard his heart still beating rapidly as they left the alley, but beyond that she had no idea how badly he was hurt.

With a short shake of her head, Kiara forced herself to stop thinking about it. She reached for her purse and pulled out her phone. Her brother answered on the first ring despite the late hour. As a paramedic, he was used to being on call.

"Cole here."

"It's me." Kiara dropped her head; the fingers of her free hand pressed into her temple. "Get up. Leave the apartment. I need you to meet us at Nathan's."

Cole didn't argue. "I'll be out in five."

"Wait." Jamie leaned forward from the backseat. "Arthur."

"It's out of the way," Kiara began.

"I've got a spare key." Her brother's voice came over the line. "Tell Dee not to worry. I'll get her dog."

Kiara gritted her teeth and hoped that his werewolf hearing wouldn't get Cole into something he couldn't get out of. "Be fast," she warned.

"Never anything but," Cole promised, as unflappable as ever, and hung up.

"Why are we going to Nathan's?"

Not for the first time, Kiara wished that Deanna had a better brain-to-mouth filter.

"Better question. Who's Nathan?" Ryn was tense in her seat beside Kiara. Her fingers drummed in an uncharacteristic show of anxiety on the side of her duffel bag. Kiara almost reached over and stilled them with her own.

"He's a friend," Kiara answered. "But he's human. I don't think they'll have made the connection."

"You don't *think*?" Deanna half rose from her seat. "Those guys—"

"Deanna!" Kiara's voice was sharp and commanding. "I'm the—" She sucked in a quick breath, reminding herself that they weren't alone in the cab. The driver was glancing in the rearview mirror with unabashed interest. "I'm the one in charge. I'm not going to let anyone get hurt. So sit still, shut up, and let me *think*."

Sullen silence greeted her, and Kiara refused to feel guilty. They'd be at Nathan's in a matter of minutes, and once they were safely inside, Deanna could ask whatever questions she could think of. Kiara wouldn't guarantee she'd *answer* them, but she wouldn't stop Deanna from asking.

Kiara tried to focus on the passing buildings as they drove through downtown, but the lights blurred until all she could see out the window was her own reflection and the shape of Ryn's profile at her side. For the first time since she'd seen Ryn onstage, Kiara let herself take in the sight of her: her stubbornly square jaw, the soft slope of her nose. She'd whipped her hair into a ponytail before they'd left the club, but a few fine tendrils had escaped to drift around her face. Though Kiara knew the glued-on beard was still in place, she couldn't see the detail of it in the window and imagined pressing her lips to the firm spot where Ryn's jaw met her throat.

She snapped her gaze away from the window as the cab slowed to a stop beside Nathan's building. She pulled out a handful of bills and passed them to the driver before she yanked open the door and stepped out. The rain was still coming down, and, as the other three followed her, Kiara was reminded that they were all soaking.

Deanna hurried past Kiara to the door with Jamie close behind. Kiara waited at the curb until the cab pulled away, then scanned the street behind them. She was fairly certain they hadn't been followed, but she wouldn't take any chances.

"So." Ryn had dropped her bag beside Jamie under the overhang and came into the rain to stand beside Kiara. "It's been a while."

Kiara wrapped her arms around herself and told herself the chill was from the weather and not from Ryn's nonchalance. "Yeah," was all she said.

"You kept the bangs."

Kiara jerked her chin in acknowledgment.

On the speaker behind them, Nathan finally answered Deanna's urgent buzzing. "Whozzit?" his sleep-muddled voice asked.

"It's Dee. Can we come in?"

The click of the door unlocking sounded louder than it should have. Kiara gave one last sweep of the road before she turned to follow Deanna and Jamie in.

Chapter Five |

THE ELEVATOR RIDE TO NATHAN'S third floor apartment was silent. Dee curled into Jamie's side; her hands were still clenched into fists. It occurred to Kiara that, unlike the three werewolves Deanna shared the elevator with, Deanna was probably drunk. If Kiara thought that the night had been an impossible whirlwind of events, she couldn't imagine how Deanna was taking it.

Before Kiara could decide if she needed to apologize, the elevator shuddered to a stop, and the doors opened with a ding. She stepped to the side to allow Deanna and Jamie to exit first, then followed. Ryn trailed behind her.

A bleary-eyed Nathan met them in his doorway and ushered them through. His dark hair was a mess, and a loose pair of pajama pants hung from his narrow hips. He didn't say a word as he closed and locked the door behind them.

Deanna had toed off her flats and was already making her way into the industrial-chic apartment. Jamie hastily unlaced her sneakers and moved into the kitchen.

Nathan eyed Kiara before his gaze shifted to Ryn and took on a speculative quality. "Hi," he said. "You're Terence Stallion."

Ryn lifted a hand to her jaw, and rubbed her facial hair. "Taryn, Ryn, now."

"Nathan. He, him," he offered.

"She or they," Ryn answered in kind, unlacing her polished oxfords.

Nathan nodded. "Make yourself at home," he said before he switched his focus to Kiara. "Care to tell me what the hell is going on?"

Kiara bent to unlace her own boots. "Cole is on his way. With Arthur."

"Right, of course. That's very informative. But *why*, pray tell, is Cole on his way with Arthur?" There was a knife-sharp edge to Nathan's voice as Kiara pried off her left boot and then her right.

"Don't be cute. You weren't my first choice, trust me," Kiara said, straightening. He wasn't her last either, but he didn't need to know that.

"And yet here you are." Nathan threw up his hands in a fashion that was far too dramatic for Kiara's taste and strode across the exposed concrete floor. "Jamie, would you mind shedding some light on this development, since your cousin is so vehemently opposed to doing so?"

Jamie sent Kiara a quick, apologetic glance and answered. "There's this group. They're not—I mean, I didn't think they were actually *real*. Or at least not anymore."

"Neither did I," Kiara responded gruffly.

"Could you all please stop being so cryptic?" Deanna had her arms folded over her chest. "I'm cold, wet, drunk, and scared and I don't know why. Could someone please just tell me what's going on?"

"I'm sorry." Ignoring Nathan's narrowed eyes, Kiara pulled a bottle of water from the fridge and joined them in the living room. Ryn had settled into a chair and was surveying the apartment with studied indifference. Kiara did her best to ignore her and focused her attention on the two humans. "We didn't have time to explain earlier." She directed her response to Deanna. "The Huntsmen are boogeymen. They're what you scare young werewolves with. You know, the baddies who'll come after them if they aren't careful. That kind of thing. They're a watchdog group of humans. Supposedly they track us down—keep you safe."

"I didn't feel safe tonight." Deanna took Jamie's hand in hers. "They attacked *us*."

"I'm sorry. You shouldn't have been caught up in that." Jamie kissed Deanna's temple before she looked up at Kiara. "What happened?"

"I don't know."

"They had to come from somewhere. Why us? Why that club?" Jamie was still directing her questions at Kiara, but Kiara didn't think she expected an answer.

"Could be them." Nathan swung his chin pointedly at Ryn. "Since we're using the 'W-word' I'm assuming they're one of yours. And, as far as I know, we haven't had problems with any kind of 'Huntsmen' until now. Until them."

"It's not Ryn." Kiara hadn't realized she was going to speak until the words flew from her mouth. She pressed her lips closed to prevent any more from exiting unbidden.

Ryn's dark eyes slid from Kiara back to Nathan, and she arched an eyebrow in his direction. "I haven't had any problems till now. Till *you*."

Nathan's own eyebrows leapt up over his glasses, but before he could respond Deanna stood up.

"I want a shower," she announced. "And Cole isn't here yet. I'm calling a time-out on this whole—" She waved a vague hand at the center of the room. "—whatever. Let me shower and sober up, and then we can continue."

"Do you want a hand?" Jamie began to rise from the couch, but Deanna shooed her back.

"I'll be fine."

"I'll get you a towel and some clothes." Nathan was already moving to the cupboards that lined one wall. "You," he directed to Jamie, "can get me a drink. Because *I* am not drunk enough for whatever werewolf nonsense this is. And especially for it to be happening at—" He squinted at the clock on the microwave. "—one in the morning."

With a sharp nod, Jamie went into the kitchen and opened cupboards. Kiara twisted the cap off her bottle and took a long drink, letting the cool liquid soothe her tight throat.

Nathan's apartment was in an old industrial building converted to lofts. The floor and walls were thick cement, making it essentially a well-furnished box. The small front entry had a bathroom to the left and a short hallway into the kitchen, which opened into a living room that ended in a large bank of windows against the far wall. A staircase ran up the apartment's right wall to Nathan's bedroom, a small second floor which extended only over the kitchen, giving the relatively small apartment tall ceilings and a wide-open feel.

On the third floor of the building, with the windows looking out into the street, the apartment's front door was the only point of entry. If need be, the apartment was easily defended.

In the bathroom the taps came on with a shuddering jerk, and the spray of water against porcelain announced Deanna had started her shower. Nathan returned to the kitchen and with a nod of thanks to Jamie he took the glass she handed him. Without a second thought, he slammed back the whiskey and slid the glass across the wooden counter for another.

"Something tells me the three of you could use one," he said.

"We're good—"

"Sure." Ignoring Kiara, Ryn rose from her chair and slid onto a barstool. Jamie avoided eye contact with Kiara as she poured Ryn a glass and passed it across before surreptitiously pouring one for herself.

Kiara closed her eyes and let out a long, slow breath through her nose. *Be calm, be calm,* she reminded herself. Jamie had—they'd both—been through something entirely unexpected this evening. If Jamie wanted a drink, Kiara supposed she was entitled to it, even if Kiara thought staying clearheaded was the best move.

Nathan's phone gave a jolting buzz from the kitchen island. Nathan's face went deathly pale at the sudden noise, but to his credit he was already answering at the second ring.

"Yeah?"

"It's Cole. And Arthur."

"Right." Nathan tapped at the screen to buzz them in, then dropped his phone on the counter with a clatter.

They waited in silence: Jamie leaning against the sink, Nathan with his elbows on the island and spinning his tumbler between his fingers, Ryn seemingly at ease with her tie askew and her own tumbler dangled carelessly above the concrete floor. Where she'd settled on the stairs, Kiara picked at the new run in her stockings and swallowed a curse when the split widened.

At the ding of the elevator reaching Nathan's floor, Jamie jerked up and sped inhuman-quick to the door. Nathan shook his head and muttered, "Fucking werewolves," before he swallowed the rest of his whiskey.

"Well," Cole rubbed a hand over his beard as he joined them in the kitchen. "You all look a mess." Despite having been roused from sleep, Cole was as put-together and unruffled as always in gray jeans and a soft, forest-green sweater that complemented his dark hair and his honey-gold eyes, which matched Kiara's.

Kiara noticed for the first time the tear in Jamie's tank top, the blood flaking against Ryn's throat, and Nathan's threadbare pajamas. She couldn't see herself, but was sure sweat had blurred her carefully applied eyeliner and mascara into dark circles, and the itchy sensation at her hairline was possibly drying blood. Deanna might have had the right idea.

Cole had clearly clued into the fact that they were waiting for Deanna; he'd pulled out a barstool beside Nathan and cracked the seal on the bottle of water Jamie had passed him.

The water in the bathroom shut off, and Arthur, who had gone to beg attention from Nathan, wagged his tail.

Deanna emerged in a billow of spice-scented steam, toweled her hair, then swooped it up into a bun. With her makeup gone, her round face looked younger, and Kiara couldn't help watching Jamie's eyes gentle as Deanna tucked herself against Jamie's side. Arthur hurried over to complete the family.

"So." Cole set down his bottle. "Now that we're all here—what's going on?" His glance slid to Ryn, but offered nothing more than polite interest in her presence.

Kiara joined the group; she stepped into the only space around the island left open, between Nathan and Ryn. She could feel the prick of Nathan's irritation against her bare arms, but on her right Ryn was a blank canvas save for the unwavering beat of her heart. She seemed unaffected, as always.

Kiara laid her palms against the wood of the island and told Cole what had happened at the club. She was blunt about the facts— including the force with which she'd thrown the Huntsman against the wall and her uncertainty as to how badly he'd been injured. From the other side of the island, Deanna's fingers worried at the hem of her T-shirt, and she flinched at Kiara's admission.

Kiara refused to feel guilty about what Deanna would see as a lie. They'd needed to leave, and Kiara had gotten them to safety, relative though it was. Kiara wouldn't apologize for whatever it took to keep her pack from harm.

"What I don't get," Jamie said with a frown, "is why we are *just* finding out the Huntsmen are real. Unless—" She hesitated, doubt, but no accusation, in her voice. "—unless Uncle Michael told you." She directed the not-quite-question to Kiara. If anyone in the room were to have knowledge of the Huntsmen, it would be Kiara, as her father's heir.

Kiara shook her head. "This is the first confirmation I've had."

Cole nodded. "Whenever Dad spoke about them, it was always past tense. Like they'd been real at one point, but not any longer."

"So." Nathan folded his arms across his chest. "Have they been around this entire time, or have they come back?"

His question hung unanswered.

"It doesn't really matter." Ryn waggled her fingers at Jamie, who passed her the bottle of whiskey, and poured herself another glass. "The point is, they're here now."

"What I think—"

"If we—"

"Listen, there's no real—"

Arthur barked, joining in.

Heedless of her already ruined makeup, Kiara pressed the heels of her hands into her eyes. Now that the immediate danger had passed, the number of questions was growing by the second. If their pack didn't know about the Huntsmen, then who did? Did GNAAW know about them? Was that all of them—the three they'd seen—or were there factions all over? How many were there? Would the Huntsmen keep coming after them? Too much to decide with too little information, and the six of them arguing in circles wouldn't help figure anything out.

"Everyone quiet!" Nathan shouted. "Especially you." He looked pointedly at Arthur. "I'm not allowed pets, so keep it down." Arthur obediently sat, and the rest of them stopped speaking.

"The way I see it." Kiara looked at each person in turn, ending with Ryn. "We stay here tonight. No question. I don't think they tracked us and I can't see them connecting us to Nathan—"

"Yet," Nathan muttered.

"—so we stay here. And I'll call my dad. And he'll know what to do."

"That's good," Cole agreed. "And I think it might be best if none of us plan on going to work tomorrow."

"Hey, no one's looking for me." Ready to argue, Nathan squared his shoulders. "I'm not missing work just because you bozos—"

"You can go to work." Kiara rolled her eyes.

"I can work wherever," Deanna reminded them. "I just need my laptop."

"Then it's settled."

"It's not settled. You can't just decide for all of us." Ryn unfurled herself from her stool. "I've got clients tomorrow. I can't reschedule."

"You can. You will," Kiara warned. "No one's going to die if they have to wait a day or two for a haircut."

"No. I'm not getting involved in this, with them, or with you." Ryn picked up her duffel bag. Kiara was on her feet in an instant.

"You're not leaving."

"I am. This isn't my mess or my problem, and *you* don't get to—"

"It is your problem! We have no idea who they were after back there. It could be one of us or it could be all of us. We don't know, and so you aren't leaving."

"Back off." Ryn's detachment had vanished, and there was a growl of warning in her words.

"Okay, whoa. Let's just bring this down for a minute." Nathan's hand was cool around Kiara's shoulder, and, with a snarl, she shook it off.

"This doesn't have anything to do with you, Nathan. Let me handle it."

"It?" Ryn's outrage mounted.

They both ignored Ryn. "It has an awful lot to do with me," Nathan argued. "If you're talking about keeping someone here, *in my apartment*, without their consent. That's unlawful confinement, or false imprisonment, whatever. If you think I'm going to let you—"

"Let me? Do you think you could stop me?"

"Hey!" Cole's voice boomed, unexpected enough to create shocked silence. "Nothing is being decided yet. Everyone take a step back, sit down, and we will discuss the best plan of action. For *all* of us."

Ryn fingered the strap of her bag, and Kiara readied, prepared to stop her if necessary. But with a sigh and an exaggerated roll of her eyes to let them know she thought it was a waste of her time, Ryn dropped the bag.

"Good. Thank you." Cole offered her a hand. "I'm Cole."

"Ryn." She shook his hand.

If Cole was surprised to hear that name, he didn't blink. Kiara stared at the wood of the kitchen cupboards across from her and tried to remember how her evening got so out of control.

"Give us tomorrow." Deanna leaned forward and appealed to Ryn. "I know it's not fair that you've been sucked up into this with us—"

"Or us into it with them," Nathan pointed out, before dodging Deanna's rebuking glance.

"—but your clients will understand you taking a sick day, right? And we'll know more tomorrow, so we can reevaluate then."

Ryn held Deanna's eyes, and the rest of them waited to hear what she'd say. Finally, Ryn dipped her chin in a nod, and relief washed over Kiara.

"I'll call Dad." Kiara stepped back from the table and retrieved her phone from her purse. Though it would make no difference to the other werewolves—and not much to the humans considering the size of his apartment—she looked at Nathan and gestured to his bedroom above them. "You mind?"

"Go ahead." Nathan ran a tired hand over his face and stared blankly at the rest of them, clearly wondering where he was going to put them all for the remainder of the night.

Kiara gave a short nod of thanks and ascended the stairs. Settling on the edge of Nathan's bed, facing away from the balcony and the rest of the apartment, she unlocked her phone and called her parents.

The landline rang and rang, until the answering machine picked up and her mother's cheery voice sounded in Kiara's ear. "You've reached the Lyons' 'den'! Sorry we can't come to the phone right now, but—" Kiara rolled her eyes and ended the call, not bothering to leave a message before calling again. Unlike their son, her parents were heavy sleepers, and she hadn't expected them to pick up at the first ring. On the third ring of the second call there was a click, and her mother's far-from-cheerful voice answered with a groggy "Kiara?"

"Hi, Mom. Is Dad there?"

Blankets rustled and then a light switch made a flicking sound before her mother replied, "It's past one in the morning. I don't know where else he'd be. Hang on, I'll put you on speaker."

Kiara's father grumbled, and Kiara heard him turn over in the bed. He was obviously unwilling to respond to her mother's hissed "Michael." The second time his name was used, accompanied, Kiara suspected, by an elbow jabbed into his side, he groaned. "What?"

"Hi, Dad." With the phone pressed to her ear, Kiara closed her eyes and felt some of the weight she'd been carrying since seeing the first tattooed axe finally ease. Her parents would know what to do, whom to talk to, how to find out what was wrong, and, most importantly, what they could do to keep themselves safe. All of them. Kiara slid down to the floor, leaned back against Nathan's bed, and explained what had happened for the third time.

Chapter Six |

As she put her phone on the floor beside her, Kiara let her head fall back against the mattress. Some of her tension had eased, but she could feel the edges of it in her temples and the base of her neck. The rest of the group was still downstairs, their voices now quiet murmurs as they settled in—such as it was—for the night. She'd have to go down, tell them what her parents had said, but for now she gave herself a moment to process: seeing her ex-girlfriend for the first time since university; learning that the monsters she'd been teased about as a child were real, and even more dangerous than she could have imagined; fighting for her life and the lives of her family, but not giving in to raw wildness; making decisions for them all because somebody had to; hoping she made the right ones.

Her hands trembled; panic closed her throat in a vise. Knowing it wouldn't take more than a second's attention for her packmates, or Ryn, to catch the spike in her pulse, Kiara forced herself to slow her breathing. *Draw it in through the count of four. Hold it for the count of four. Release through the count of seven. Repeat. Repeat. Repeat.*

The meditation technique helped, and her heartbeat slowed. The voices from downstairs hadn't paused, so if anyone had noticed they'd given her the privacy she'd sought.

Having delayed long enough, Kiara picked up her phone and rejoined the others. She had to stop at the foot of the stairs to step over Arthur, who was golden, content, and oblivious.

"He wants us to sit tight. He'll contact GNAAW, the emergency line." The General North American Assembly of Werewolves handled any emergencies or politics that might occur. They kept the existence of werewolves secret and scrubbed what they could from the Internet and from police reports. If anyone knew anything about the Huntsmen, really knew about them, not the rumors Kiara and her brother and their cousin had heard growing up, it would be GNAAW.

"So, what? We just wait for the authorities to tell us what to do?" The sarcasm in Ryn's voice was palpable, and she emphasized it with a curled lip.

"Can you not?" Though she'd told herself to be patient, to act as though the other werewolf was a total stranger, Kiara rose too easily to the bait and glowered at Ryn, who had taken the time to step into the washroom to clean the beard off. Seeing the whole of Ryn's face, bare and familiar, twisted Kiara's heart into a painful knot.

"Ryn's got a point." Nathan came from the kitchen and passed Cole a steaming cup of tea. "Is that really all we can do?"

"This isn't something any of us have experience with," Jamie reminded them. "You weren't there, Nathan, but these guys mean business. They're not a joke, or a single dude with a grudge. They're organized. They're smart. And they knew what we were."

"Then they knew what they were getting into." For the first time since the alleyway, Deanna met Kiara's eyes with her own, sincere and steady. It was an apology and a show of understanding, so Kiara's next words came a bit more easily.

"My dad will call us when he knows more. But for now..." She shrugged and directed her next question to Nathan. "Do you have any spare blankets or sleeping bags?"

"I have a sleeping bag in the car," Cole offered. At everyone else's surprised and puzzled looks, he gave an unselfconscious shrug. "Paramedic," he offered. "It pays to be prepared."

"Great. Good. Yeah." Nathan looked around the room. His normally sharp blue eyes were still fuzzy, whether due to the late hour or the events he'd been dragged into, Kiara wasn't sure. "You wanna grab it?"

Cole nodded and rose from the couch, after carefully setting his mug of tea on a coaster. "Sure."

"No." Kiara shook her head. "We can't leave. We don't know where the Huntsmen are or if they were able to track us. None of us—" She gestured to the three other werewolves. "—can leave. Not until we know more." *I'm sorry,* she wanted to add, but it wouldn't do any good.

Ryn rolled her eyes, Jamie nodded, and Cole pulled his keys from his pocket and held them out to Nathan.

"What?" Nathan blinked, uncomprehending.

"If you don't mind going instead?" Cole gave an apologetic shrug. "I'm across the road and down the street a block. Vancouver," he added by way of explanation.

"I can go with you." Deanna began to rise.

"They saw you earlier," Jamie reminded her.

"Right." Deanna sank down and mouthed a "sorry" to Nathan.

"So I'll just walk a block, in the middle of the night, in my pajamas, to get you a sleeping bag," Nathan clarified. "I'll just do that. Me. On my own."

"If you wouldn't mind." Patiently, Cole continued to hold out the keys. With a long-suffering sigh, Nathan plucked them from Cole's hand and walked toward the door. He stopped at the closet to pull out a jacket. Sensing a walk, Arthur scrabbled to his feet.

"There." Deanna quirked a grin at Nathan. "Now you won't be alone. Arthur will go with you."

Nathan gave an exaggerated sigh as Arthur skidded toward him on the concrete floor.

"His leash is on the hanger with my coat," Cole called. Nathan raised his hand in a thank you. He grabbed his house keys from the counter, yanked the leash from the hanger, and strode out the door with a golden retriever hot on his heels.

"Come on." Deanna yawned and stood up from the couch. "I know where he keeps the air mattress. If we start pumping now we should be done by the time he gets back."

Jamie followed Deanna up the stairs, and Cole was already moving the coffee table out of the way. Kiara stepped back, neither knowing the apartment nor feeling comfortable enough to move Nathan's furniture—unlike her brother, apparently. She knew Jamie spent a lot of time with Nathan, as he was Deanna's best friend, and the two of them were practically glued at the hip. She frowned, trying to decide whether the ease with which Cole was making himself at home was due to familiarity with the space, or simply because Cole was generally at ease.

The question was another to add to the night's long list, and Kiara decided to drop it.

"I'm going to go out for some air."

"You said we couldn't leave," was Ryn's sharp reminder.

"Not out front," Kiara clarified, unwilling or unable—she wasn't going to examine that right now either—to meet Ryn's eyes. "Up."

Cole nodded, a little too understanding. Kiara grabbed her purse and fled, picking up her boots on the way out. Putting them on in the doorway would make her feel too vulnerable.

Once Nathan's front door closed, she pulled on the boots. With her purse on her shoulder, and again wishing she hadn't left her coat at the club, Kiara moved down the hallway to the stairs.

Chapter Seven |

SHE KNEW HER WAY TO the roof. Nathan had shown her, months ago, when Kiara and Cole had first relocated to Vancouver. He'd thrown a party and insisted they all come. Not liking parties full of strangers, Kiara had tried her best to get out of it, but somehow Deanna had popped by with Jamie for "just a quick drink beforehand," and the next thing Kiara knew she was crammed into Nathan's loft with her back against the wall and her beer brandished in front of her like a shield as the bass pounded through her bones.

"Not much for crowds, eh?" Nathan had leaned against the wall beside her. Behind his glasses, his eyes were bright and his pupils blown wide as he took a draw from the vaporizer in his hand. There were two vivid lipstick prints on his cheek, one bright red and the other even brighter pink. Kiara took a drink of her beer to hide her amusement.

"Not much, no." She shrugged. "Everyone else is having a good time, though." She nodded to where Cole was engrossed in a shouted conversation with Isabel and Darren, an attractive Black couple.

Nathan hummed. "I'd worried about Jamie; she can be kinda shy, but…" Kiara followed Nathan's gesture and snorted. Jamie and Deanna had claimed a corner of the black leather couch and were making out enthusiastically. Kiara suspected that, when they surfaced, the lipstick smeared over Jamie's lips would match one of the prints on Nathan's cheek.

"You want to get some air?" Nathan asked.

Kiara blew out a grateful breath. "Yes."

"Come on." He tugged her away from the wall. "I know just the place."

"Well, I'll say this for Vancouver: you can't beat the view," Kiara commented when Nathan led her onto the roof. Nathan's place was close enough to downtown that the view of the high-rises lit up at night, with the mountains towering in the background, was stunning, but not close enough to downtown that the noise was unbearable. In fact, with his human senses, Nathan probably couldn't hear it at all.

"Why'd you come?" Nathan leaned against the edge of the roof with his back to the incredible view and looked at Kiara with eyes that were shrewd despite the weed.

Kiara shrugged. "Jamie was here; Cole was coming. I couldn't not." Despite Nathan's suspicious personality—or maybe because of it— Kiara liked him.

"They're important to you," Nathan observed.

"They're pack," Kiara said. That should have been enough. It helped that she liked her brother and her cousin, of course, but at the very core, it was that simple: They were pack.

"Well, Dee is *my* pack." Nathan met her gaze full-on. "She's what's important to me; the most important. This whole werewolf thing is beyond intense. And she loves Jamie so much that she's wrapped up in it for good now. So you'd better protect her from this shit, okay? We were on our own last year and we could have died. One of your kind *stalked* Deanna. I've never been so scared." He paused; his nostrils flared as he tried to get his emotions under control. "I love Dee more than anything, and if she gets hurt again I will come after you. Maybe that's not fair, but I will. I'm making you personally responsible. Dee, she's... she's the best of us. You keep her safe."

Kiara let her gaze fall to the cityscape, and sipped her beer. "I understand." Nathan, she thought, would make a good wolf.

"Good." Nathan let out a breath. "Thank you."

☾

WHEN SHE STEPPED OUT ONTO the roof, some of the tension Kiara had been holding onto all evening relaxed. Though she hadn't been in Nathan's apartment long, just a little over two hours, the air inside had been stifling—too many people in too small a space. It would only get worse. But out here on the rooftop, with the view of downtown a blaze of lights to her left and the unassuming, less high-rise-style housing to her right, Kiara could breathe again.

She walked to the edge and eased a hip against the ledge. She pulled a crumpled pack of mentholated slims from her purse. They were probably stale, but she couldn't bring herself to care.

With a disgusted noise, she dropped her purse to the rooftop. Her lighter was in her leather coat—the same leather coat she'd left in the coat check at the bar. She was sure Nathan would have a lighter or matches, but the thought of going downstairs to ask was decidedly unappealing.

"Here."

Kiara should have heard Ryn approach, and maybe a part of her had, a part that she'd ignored. She bent and inhaled as Ryn held the flame to the tip of the cigarette.

"You smoke now?" Kiara asked, in lieu of thanks.

"No." Ryn tucked the lighter into her pocket.

Kiara took a deep draw from the cigarette. The cool mentholated smoke hit the back of her throat and expanded in her lungs before she let it slide lazily from her parted lips. She'd quit years ago. Mostly. Almost. But the act of smoking, focusing on air going in and out of her lungs, relaxed her. And so she kept a pack on hand. Meditation helped for a while, and she practiced yoga a few times a week, but nothing gave her the same instant sense of calm as the first familiar draw from a cigarette.

"Why did you follow me?" she asked, looking out over the city. Oxfords scuffing against the gravel as she settled, Ryn leaned against the roof ledge beside her.

"Do you really want me to answer that?"

Kiara looked over. "Yes."

Ryn's hand circled the back of Kiara's neck and brought their lips together. Kiara swayed into it; the feel of Ryn's soft lips against hers was as heady as the smoke. Ryn pressed deeper, her tongue sliding between Kiara's parted lips, and Kiara heard herself whimper. "For this," Ryn kissed her again, harder. Kiara dropped the cigarette, and her hands rose to grasp the crisp fabric of Ryn's dress shirt to drag her closer.

"And this," Ryn mouthed down Kiara's jaw; her teeth sank in when she found the bend of Kiara's neck. Kiara let out a swift, vicious curse, wrapped her legs around Ryn, and pulled her closer until the jut of Ryn's hips dug into the soft flesh of Kiara's thighs where her dress had ridden up.

Kiara's head was spinning with adrenaline, whiskey, nicotine, and Ryn. The cause didn't matter. Kiara didn't care. All she cared about was the heat building between her legs and the desperate, uncaring need that swept through her like a storm. "Fuck me," she demanded, pulling at Ryn's shirt as Ryn's hands skimmed down her thighs to lift her from the ledge and stagger to a bench.

Ryn's hot hands cupped her ass through the fine mesh of Kiara's ruined stockings and the smooth silk of her underwear. As Ryn spilled her onto the bench, those same hands tore carelessly through the hose, pushed the silk aside, and drove into Kiara. A moan ripped from her as she arced into the sensation; her fingers scrabbled for purchase against the smoothness of Ryn's skin.

"Don't stop," she begged, shameless.

"I won't." Ryn bent her head and dragged her lips over the mounds of Kiara's breasts where they showed above her dress. "I won't," she promised, her fingers moving ceaselessly inside of Kiara as Kiara shook and trembled around her.

Her hips rising mindlessly, desperately, to meet Ryn's thrusts, Kiara grabbed fistfuls of Ryn's hair and dragged her head up to find Ryn's lips with hers. As the first orgasm ripped through her, she moaned into Ryn's mouth and felt Ryn's lips pull into a wide smile as she brought Kiara to her second orgasm.

"It's not enough." Kiara's chest heaved as she tried to suck in enough air despite the sensations driving her breathless. "I need more. Give me more." A sob fell from her lips. She wanted to feel Ryn everywhere: inside her, around her, under her, and on top of her until there was nothing but Ryn, until everything disappeared except the thunder of Ryn's heart against hers and the sound of their ragged breathing and moving bodies.

As Ryn pressed another finger into her, Kiara worked her hand down between them, wriggling past Ryn's belt until she hit the hot, taut skin underneath.

"Can I?" she asked, her voice strung with urgency.

In their past, Ryn had experienced some feelings related to gender dysphoria. She'd expressed to Kiara that she didn't feel like a woman any more than she felt like a man, and that sometimes—especially during sex, perhaps because standard social scripts relied so heavily on heteronormative gender roles—she felt anxious, frustrated, and alienated from her body. After she'd learned that, Kiara tried to be especially careful to affirm Ryn's boundaries and to check if she was uncertain. Ten years wasn't going to change that.

"Yes." Ryn moaned as Kiara's fingertips brushed the coarse thatch of hair between her thighs, and Kiara pushed farther, fingers dipping into the wet heat and rubbing frantically at Ryn's clit until Ryn's hips thrust against Kiara in time with Ryn's fingers inside of her.

Kiara convulsed around Ryn for a third time as Ryn went rigid above her. Ryn's forehead dug into the bend of Kiara's neck as the two of them rode the crest before Ryn collapsed on top of her, and Kiara fell bonelessly into the bench.

Ryn's heart beat against Kiara's. Kiara brought a weak hand up to cup the back of Ryn's head and hold her close.

It had started to rain. Kiara wasn't sure when, but the cool drops—not a torrent, but a gentle breaking of the storm—were a counterpoint to the heat of Ryn's bare skin under her arms.

"It won't be enough." Ryn pulled herself up, and the loss of her left an ache. Kiara was suddenly aware of the wooden bench, uncomfortable against her back, and of the awkward angle of her leg. She was cold, now. It didn't have anything to do with her forgotten jacket.

Not sure of what to say to Ryn, not trusting her voice, she pushed herself to her feet and crossed the roof to her purse. Her cigarette had gone out in the gravel, and the rain had rendered what was left of it—a good half—unsalvageable. She picked it up anyway, unwilling to litter Nathan's rooftop, and tucked it into her purse as she pulled out the pack.

"You should quit," Ryn called, careless of the way her long hair hung disheveled and her pants rode low on her hips.

"You always say that," Kiara reminded her. She walked back, bent, and pressed the cigarette tip to the light Ryn offered. Old patterns returned, like breathing. A person could only stop for so long before being forced back into it.

Drawing the smoke into her mouth, Kiara dropped to the bench beside Ryn and crossed one leg over the other.

Ryn didn't turn to face her, but gazed out at the cityscape. The rain still fell gently, and the tip of Kiara's cigarette glowed brightly in the darkness.

With her body still thrumming from Ryn's touch, Kiara felt the first moment of peace, real, true peace, in years. It sank into her bones like a hot bath, and she let herself settle into it. Ryn always had that effect on her—she made Kiara forget everything.

"I'm sorry," Kiara said abruptly. "I know you don't want to be here. I know you have your own life in Vancouver." *Without me.*

"I do," Ryn agreed. Her arm rested on the bench behind Kiara, and Kiara refused to lean back, despite everything in her that cried for the concession. She wasn't ruled by this, by Ryn, anymore. That wasn't who she was now.

"I didn't know you were here." Kiara thought it was important to say. True. If she *had* known she'd be moving to the same city as her ex-lover, Kiara wouldn't have come. No matter that Jamie was here, no matter that the job offer—working with one of Vancouver's largest construction companies—had been incredible. She'd have come up with an excuse—no, a legitimate reason. Something so solid that no one would have questioned her refusal.

Ryn shifted on the bench beside her and withdrew her arm from where it had been almost around Kiara. "I figured."

"Not that—I mean—" Kiara stumbled over the words. She flicked the ash from her cigarette with a casual tap of her thumb. "You're happy here. You looked happy, onstage. I'm glad."

"I am," Ryn replied easily. "This is a good city. Good people."

"It's just you, though?"

Out of the corner of her eye, she caught the quick flash of Ryn's grin, but refused to look.

"I'm never short of lovers, if that's what you're asking."

"I'm not." Kiara's response was too short, too sharp, and belied her denial. "I mean you don't have a pack," she clarified.

"No."

That was another thing that hadn't changed. Ryn had been adopted as a baby. She had shifted for the first time at puberty, as most young werewolves did, but she had done it on her own. She'd had no preparation for the changes her body went through. Her only context for the experience had come from paranormal novels and horror movies.

When Kiara met her in college, Ryn was a biracial, genderqueer eighteen-year-old, politically outspoken and personally unapologetic.

Her lone wolf persona was an intrinsic part of her. She found Kiara's attachment and unyielding obedience to her pack unfathomable and steadfastly refused each of Kiara's attempts to explain the importance of pack.

"Is there any reason why… I mean, have you—does anyone *know*?" There were reasons lone wolves weren't celebrated by werewolf society. Without a pack, werewolves had no one to turn to when they ran into trouble, had questions, or simply grew exhausted with the weight of their secret. A lone wolf was more likely to be so desperate for companionship, for someone they could share everything with, that they spilled their secrets without knowing they would be kept safe.

Kiara didn't know if it was the human or wolf part of them that craved belonging. She wasn't sure it mattered, in the end.

"I keep my secrets, Kiara."

"The Huntsmen had to know from somewhere."

"I didn't tell anyone. I'm careful. No one knew before you. No one's known after." The bitterness in Ryn's voice dug like a knife into Kiara's side, and it took all she had not to flinch away from it. "Besides," Ryn continued. "It's not hard for one person to keep a secret. But five?" She twisted to face Kiara. "Five is a lot of people."

"We didn't tell anyone who isn't in that room downstairs."

"But were you careful? As careful as you should be?" Ryn's accusations were sharp, as if that same knife, lodged in Kiara's side, were twisting. "You're sure none of you grew complacent, secure in the fact that you can always just run back to Daddy when you get in trouble?"

Indignation sucked the air from Kiara's lungs. Ryn didn't wait for her to regain her footing, but simply stood.

"All I'm saying is, watch your glass house. Those are some big stones you're throwing."

The door clanged shut behind Ryn. The sudden silence hung in the air, as uncomfortable as the sweat drying cold against Kiara's skin.

It hadn't been her pack. She was certain. They were smart; they had grown up in this world, had the rules drilled into them before they could tie their own shoelaces. Neither she, nor Jamie, nor Cole would be so reckless as to let something slip.

Would they?

Doubt added a twist to her stomach, a weight to her shoulders.

The rain was coming harder now. Kiara rose from the bench. She'd raid Nathan's closet for something more comfortable than her dress and wait to hear from her father.

Which, she reminded herself, annoyed by the necessity, was not the same thing as running back to Daddy.

Downstairs, Ryn had locked Nathan's front door behind her. Even though Kiara knew it was the smart, safe, thing to do, lifting her hand to knock rankled. Jamie answered a moment later, but instead of swinging the door open to let Kiara in, she stepped out. Kiara was forced to back up or let Jamie run into her.

As Jamie eased the door shut, Kiara clenched her jaw, anticipating the question a heartbeat before it came out of Jamie's mouth.

"Are you okay?" Jamie's voice was soft, and Kiara found the concern in her honey-gold eyes, just a shade darker than Kiara's own, oppressive.

"I'm fine," Kiara snapped. They were both keeping their voices low, barely over a whisper. It wasn't for the sake of Nathan's neighbors, who were surely asleep at two or three in the morning, but because they were well aware that the thin barrier of the door would do little to hide their conversation from Ryn and Cole.

Jamie rolled her eyes. "You are not." Her nose wrinkled as she took a deliberate sniff of the air. "Don't think I don't know what you two were doing up there."

"Let me shower then, would you?" Kiara tried to step around Jamie, but Jamie's arm reached out and blocked her. Kiara could have moved her—it wouldn't have been easy, but she could have done it. Instead, she stepped back. "It's nothing. It's… old flames reuniting. It's what it always was with us. All flash and bang and no weight."

"Kiara." The softness was back in Jamie's voice, hinting at a gentle understanding that left Kiara prickly.

"Don't," Kiara warned. "Don't. This isn't you and Deanna; this isn't something worth meddling in. Just let me inside so I can shower and we can go to bed."

Jamie reluctantly dropped her hand and let Kiara pass.

Inside, Kiara ducked into the bathroom immediately to the left of the doorway. Someone, Deanna, she suspected, had left a stack of fresh towels on top of the toilet. Grateful that she wouldn't have to hunt one down, Kiara pulled off her clothes and stepped into the shower.

WRAPPED IN A TOWEL AND a billow of steam, Kiara stepped out of the bathroom. She expected to see Nathan's living room transformed—the furniture pushed against the walls, pillows and bedding strewn across the floor—but nothing seemed to have changed. In fact, all five people seemed to have vanished.

She cocked her head and focused—for the most part she did her best to ignore her enhanced senses. Reacting to things normal humans couldn't hear, smell, or feel tended to make those normal humans uncomfortable, so she and the other werewolves had learned at a young age to let the extrasensory details wash over them.

Now that she focused, she caught slow, even breathing above her. There was a soft rustle of sheets, Nathan sleepily mumbling, "Quit hogging the covers," and Cole's quiet grunt as Nathan reclaimed what covers he could.

She must have been in the shower for longer than she'd realized, if everyone had gone up to bed already. Moving quietly, Kiara crossed into the kitchen where someone—probably, again, Deanna—had left a folded pair of men's sweat pants and a ratty T-shirt. Grateful for the change of clothes, Kiara changed and hung the towel to dry before she went up the stairs.

Though some light filtered in from downstairs, the loft was mostly dark. On the bed, Nathan was curled up on one side, while Cole sprawled across the other. On an air mattress beside the bed, Jamie was wrapped around Deanna, who looked up to meet Kiara's eyes.

"We decided to keep all the beds in one place. Are you okay with the couch downstairs?" Deanna kept her voice low. "You're the only person short enough to really fit on it comfortably, and Ryn…"

In the corner Ryn had burrowed into a borrowed sleeping bag. Her back was to Kiara and the rest of the room, and, despite what Kiara was sure was an abundance of pillows, her head rested on her duffel bag, as if she was afraid someone would take it.

"It's fine."

"There's some more sheets and a blanket downstairs, I left them on the armchair. Do you need—" Deanna started to move, but Jamie's arms tightened around her waist, and even in the dark Kiara could see Deanna's fond smile.

"I'm good. Go to sleep." As quietly as she'd come up the stairs, Kiara glided down them.

Chapter Eight |

TEN YEARS AGO...

Kiara tried to keep a lid on her annoyance as she climbed the stairs in a stranger's house. She wasn't sure whose house it was and she did not intend to spend another thirty minutes downstairs waiting while Sophia hooked up with the smug asshole from their Intro to Anthropology class. She could tell that Sophia was still in the house; she could just make out the sound of her voice—breathy and excited—over the impossibly loud bass. Why her only friend at the University of Alberta thought it was a good idea to lose her virginity to some jackass who thought a thrift store vest was cutting edge was beyond Kiara, but she'd wanted to support Sophia's choices. And, if she was being honest, she trusted nothing about the university party scene.

She'd been happy—well not happy, but not actively against—coming along, at least until the third frat boy had spilled beer on her new top in a pathetic attempt to hit on her. At that point, the bright sequins on her shirt counteracting the dark snarl on her face, she'd made up her mind that it was time to go home. And since there was no way in hell she was leaving Sophia behind, Kiara had resolved to drag her friend with her, unless Sophia was still in the middle of *things*—despite all evidence to the contrary, Kiara wasn't a monster—but she was fairly certain that unless whiskey-dick had hit Smug Asshole, Sophia had long since done what she'd come to do.

Kiara spared a moment to knock on the closed bedroom door before she twisted the knob and shoved it open, deliberately keeping her eyes down. "Okay, Soph, let's—"

"K! Oh , my god, look how cute I am!" Sophie's excited squeal wasn't exactly what Kiara had been expecting, but she gamely looked up, gritting her teeth in anticipation of whatever she might find.

She had a moment of thanks that Sophia wasn't naked astride Smug Asshole and another of complete confusion. Sophia's long, impossibly straight red hair had been lopped off, and she was preening with a pixie cut in front of a full-length mirror.

"I—what?" Kiara stared, baffled. Where was Smug Asshole? What had happened?

"Suits her, right?" Kiara's eyes snapped from Sophia to the person lolling in the doorway of the en suite bathroom. She wasn't sure why she hadn't noticed them before, and Kiara's nostrils flared just slightly as she instinctively scented the air.

Warm leather, orange peel, and the sweetness of clove overlaid the crisp, sharp scent of pine. Kiara's eyes widened; her pulse skipped a beat as like recognized like.

A wry grin tugged the lips of the Korean girl in the doorway, and she moved forward with her hand extended to Kiara. "I'm Ryn."

"I know it's a huge change," Sophia was babbling, mostly to herself, as she turned this way and that in front of the mirror. "But I love it. At first I was like, 'Um, no, don't touch my hair!' But then Ryn told me that I have the perfect neck for this, and honestly, K, I think she's right. Like, not to brag, but." Sophia ran her fingers over the back of her neck, exposed for the first time, and beamed. "I look so hot."

"Kiara," Kiara murmured absently as she placed her hand in Ryn's. Ryn's hand was warm, and though Kiara had expected a quick shake, Ryn kept ahold of her hand. Kiara could have pulled free. She doubted

Ryn would make a show of the strength they both knew she had, but Ryn drew her closer and, despite herself, Kiara followed.

"Let me do you."

"What?" Incredulity sharpened Kiara's voice.

"Your hair." Ryn reached out. It took everything Kiara had to remain still. Her pulse hammered as Ryn gently pushed Kiara's dark hair out of her face. "You have amazing eyes." Ryn's hand lingered on the shell of Kiara's ear as she tucked the offending hair behind it. "You shouldn't hide them. Let me cut your hair."

"I'm not—I just met—this is a *party*," Kiara stuttered.

"This is what I do," Ryn's voice was warm, amused, and something about it was oddly reassuring. To be, after over a month, finally around someone who was her own kind dissolved Kiara's resistance. What was the risk, really? Hair grew back.

"Come on, K! Let her, let her!" Sophia chanted.

Kiara's hand was still caught in Ryn's, and, without dropping her gaze from Ryn's, Kiara gave a slow nod of assent.

☾

KIARA HURRIED OUT OF FUNDAMENTALS of Fluid Mechanics with her mind already focused on the assignment she had to complete for next week. She'd have to trade in the textbook she currently carried for another one and opted to make the detour to her locker now instead of after her last class of the day.

She rounded the corner and came up short. Ryn leaned nonchalantly against Kiara's locker with her hands tucked in the pockets of a battered black peacoat. Kiara's free hand flew up, suddenly self-conscious, to her hair. She'd tried but she hadn't managed to style it as well as Ryn had done.

"Don't worry," Ryn said with a cocky grin. "You look incredible."

Kiara flushed, heat in her cheeks and the hollow of her throat. After she had finished Kiara's hair, Ryn had given Kiara her number and told her to call. Kiara hadn't. She'd tried to; she'd pulled out her phone and stared at it with her finger hovering over the call button, but couldn't find the nerve to press down. What would she say? She'd never met someone like Ryn. Days later, Kiara could still feel the sure touch of Ryn's fingers in her hair. She'd woken up more than one night since with the ghost of those fingers gliding along the nape of her neck, with her body hot and throbbing with the ache of unfulfilled desire.

Ryn pushed off the locker, and her coat slid open to reveal her T-shirt with the words "EAT FUCK HOWL" emblazoned in all caps.

A disbelieving laugh fell from Kiara's lips.

Ryn shrugged, the movement languid and graceful. "I thought you might want to join me for the first. Then maybe we can see about the other two."

Kiara's skin tightened; her breath caught in her throat.

"Unless you have class or something." Ryn nodded at the textbook Kiara carried.

"I—" She did, Intro to Anthropology with Sophie. But it was an elective, and she could get the notes from Sophie tomorrow. "No." Kiara decided, recklessly. "No, I don't have class."

☾

RYN'S FINGERS MOVED INSIDE KIARA with incredible speed. Kiara arched off the bed with her skin sheened in sweat and her hands clenched on the bedsheets. Ryn pressed her hand against Kiara's bucking hips, strong, stronger than any lover Kiara had had. Ryn's dark eyes flashed as she panted above Kiara; her long hair fanned down around them. Kiara could still taste Ryn on her lips, on her tongue.

Ryn pushed another finger inside Kiara, and Kiara came with a cry. Body still pulsing from the orgasm, Kiara turned the tables on Ryn, using her own inhuman strength to flip them so now Ryn was splayed against the scarlet bedsheets.

Ryn laughed, breathless and delighted. "It's never been like this. I've never—" She broke off as Kiara drew a nipple into her mouth and nipped at the peaked flesh.

"It's different with us," Kiara murmured against Ryn's skin as she slid down Ryn's body, already anticipating another taste of the slick wetness between Ryn's legs. "With another wolf."

The thrill of it burned fire-hot in her veins. Like Ryn, Kiara had never slept with another werewolf—everyone she knew was family, pack—but she'd heard enough from her older cousins. Ryn, though… Ryn had never *met* another werewolf.

Kiara found Ryn's clit, and Ryn moaned, thrashing under Kiara's tongue. Kiara growled, a deep, wolfish rumble that vibrated against Ryn's most sensitive places. Ryn cried out and convulsed.

"Again," she demanded. "Again."

☾

Kiara burrowed deeper into the blankets, doing her best to ignore the weak winter sun that filtered through the blinds. She was warm and languid and had been dozing on and off for what seemed like hours. She knew the bedroom floor would be freezing against her bare feet and so had decided that she wasn't going to get out of bed until she had absolutely no other choice.

"Don't you have class today?" Ryn asked. She flicked through one of Kiara's engineering textbooks. Kiara had brought it over two nights ago, meaning to study while Ryn did a client's hair. Kiara hadn't left since, nor had she managed to crack the book open.

"I do." Kiara yawned and snuggled closer to Ryn under the covers, not bothering to open her eyes. "But I'd rather stay here."

"Won't your parents get mad though? Your *Alpha*?" Ryn mocked lightly. She tossed the book to the floor.

"Mmm, only if I tell them." Kiara propped her chin in her hands. "And I don't plan on telling them."

"Ooh, does that mean I'm your dirty little secret?" Ryn teased, toying with Kiara's new bangs. "Don't want to let the folks know you're slumming it with the loners?"

Kiara rolled her eyes. "It's not that." She traced the skin on Ryn's arm and watched as goosebumps rose in her wake. "And just because you don't have a pack doesn't mean you're a loner, just that you're a lone."

"Alone," Ryn rolled the word around on her tongue.

"No, not alone, *a lone*," Kiara clarified. "A lone wolf." She took Ryn's hand and linked their fingers together.

"I'm not alone right now." Her lips soft and warm, Ryn kissed Kiara. "Especially if you're ditching class again."

"He posts all the slides online anyway," Kiara murmured against Ryn's mouth. She already felt herself getting wet as Ryn tugged the sheets down to expose her.

"Oh, well, in that case…" Ryn trailed her hand down Kiara's stomach. "Why don't I propose a different syllabus?"

Chapter Nine |

"Why can't he just use filters, like normal people?" Kiara asked under her breath as she poked unhappily at what she assumed was Nathan's coffee maker. It sat on the counter in front of her, too shiny and modern, and she wanted to punch it. Beside it stood a tall metal rack full of incomprehensible plastic pods.

There had to be some way, other than using the terrifying machine in front of her, to get the hot water on top of the coffee grounds and filter it into a cup. Having slept fitfully, with one eye open and angled toward the door all night, Kiara wasn't willing to start the day without coffee.

"Defeated by technology?" Stifling a yawn, Nathan came down the stairs. Kiara scowled, tugging self-consciously at the hem of her T-shirt.

"Not defeated," Kiara argued. A person couldn't be defeated by an inanimate object.

"Uh huh," Nathan agreed, patently humoring her. "It usually doesn't hurt to turn it on." He tapped an unremarkable round button on the side, and the machine in front of her coughed. Kiara edged away, let Nathan fuss with it, and passed him a mug from the cupboard when he waggled impatient fingers.

"Cream, sugar?" he asked when the machine gave a final, menacing hiss and the stream of steaming hot coffee sputtered to a stop.

"Please."

Nathan opened the fridge and passed her a small carton of cream before he bent to rummage in a drawer. Finally, with a beam of triumph, he pulled out a tiny packet of sugar—the kind found at a crappy diner—and tossed it her way.

"Thanks," was Kiara's grudging reply as she tore off the top and let the grains spill into her cup. Left to her own devices she'd pour sugar straight from the bowl, but given the dubious nature of the now-empty packet in her hands, she resigned herself to sugar-free coffee going forward.

Nathan stuck his own mug in the machine, and the process started all over again. Kiara suppressed a shudder of distaste and eased out of the kitchen to stand on the other side of the island.

"Thank you, again, for letting us stay here," she said stiffly. It was no small favor, and she wanted him to know that it was appreciated.

Cupping his mug—WORLD'S BEST LIBRARIAN, it proclaimed cheerfully—Nathan shrugged. "I don't mind the company, though usually I prefer it arrives *before* midnight."

Kiara nodded and took a sip of the coffee. It could be sweeter, but wasn't half bad.

Movement at the doorway of the apartment brought Kiara's attention to Arthur, who looked up at both of them with something approaching desperation.

"Oops." Nathan set down his mug. "I'd better take him out. B-R-B!"

"Be right back" has the same number of syllables, Kiara thought grumpily. She took her coffee and walked across the room to the large windows that made up the far wall. The rain was still falling; the sky was a miserable gray. Peering down, she could make out Nathan as he emerged from the building with a blue hoodie clutched tightly under his chin. Arthur danced along the sparse grass beside him.

The rain muffled some of the noise from street, but she could hear the light cadence of Nathan's voice as he spoke to Arthur and the rumble of traffic in the distance. Footsteps approached; two figures headed toward Nathan and Arthur. Kiara tensed and pressed closer to the cold pane of the window. But the two people passed Nathan and Arthur without incident, and Kiara forced herself to stand down.

Bare feet slapped on the stairs behind her. Kiara turned and promptly wished she hadn't.

"Good morning, sunshine." Ryn wore nothing but her white button-up from the night before, and Kiara's face heated at the glimpse of her long legs. She turned to the window.

"Did you sleep well?" Ryn asked. Kiara made a noncommittal noise. She heard Ryn open cupboards until she found the mugs and then the coffee maker came back to life. The noise flooded the apartment. Aware that she couldn't keep staring out the window forever, especially now that Nathan and Arthur were out of sight, Kiara took a long swallow of her coffee and went to the kitchen.

"There's no sugar."

"Aw, don't say that, love—you're sweet enough for me." Flirting came to Ryn as easily as breathing, and Kiara refused to let it get to her. Besides, both of them knew that Kiara was anything but sweet.

Ryn rummaged in the fridge until she found the cream. Gesturing at the apartment, she asked, "How long have you known him?"

"A while. Jamie has known him longer. He helped, last year, with the rogue."

Ryn's brow furrowed. "The rogue?"

"Deanna works for *Wolf's Run*, you know, the mobile game where humans pretend to be werewolves, so they can claim territory or whatever."

"Seriously?" Ryn grinned. "I love that app."

Of course she did. "Right, well, over the summer she started getting harassed. Someone with the username 'crywolf' sent her threatening messages and then mail. He said he was actually a werewolf, and that the game was upsetting. Obviously no one believed him."

"Obviously."

"But Jamie clued in—so then she had to tell Dee, because she didn't think Dee was taking his threats seriously enough. He came after Dee and some of the other game players. Nathan and Dee and Jamie held him off until Cole and I could get there. And then we were able to pass him off to GNAAW."

"Do you know what happened to him?"

"To who?"

"Crywolf. Do you know what they did with him?"

Kiara shook her head, baffled. "GNAAW has him. He won't hurt anyone again."

"You're not even the least bit curious? You don't want to know where they took him? Or if he's still alive?" Ryn pushed off the counter with disgust written in every line of her body. "I thought maybe you'd get over the unquestioning obedience at some point. I guess not."

"Not everything has to be questioned, Taryn. Not everything needs to be fought against."

Ryn gave a quiet laugh. "That's how you've always seen it—as fighting against something. It's not what I'm fighting against, Kiara, it's what I'm fighting *for*. It's too bad you've never found anything worth it."

Kiara's mouth snapped open, but the sound of more footsteps on the stairs had her biting her tongue.

"Morning." Deanna yawned, raking a hand through her mess of curls. "Everyone sleep okay?"

Jamie came down the stairs behind her, carefully avoided making eye contact with either Kiara or Ryn, and made a beeline for the coffee.

"Fine," Kiara responded shortly. Ryn sauntered past her into the living room, where she sprawled over one end of the couch.

"Nathan take Arthur out?" Deanna asked as Jamie handed her a cup.

Kiara nodded. "There's no sugar."

Deanna made a face, but didn't complain further as she took a drink. Jamie found orange juice in the fridge and poured herself a tall glass. The three of them stood around the island. Jamie and Deanna exchanged uncomfortable looks. Kiara snuck a look at Ryn out of the corner of her eye. Ryn had set her mug on the window ledge and tipped her head against the wall behind her. She looked completely comfortable, and Kiara hated her.

"If there's no sugar, I'll take some of that juice." Cole wandered down to join them. Unlike the rest of them he'd had the chance to grab a change of clothes, and his Teagan and Sara *Love You to Death* tour shirt fit him comfortably. Kiara thought she might hate him, too.

As Cole put the juice into the fridge, the front door opened. Deanna jumped—unlike the three werewolves, she hadn't heard the elevator doors open or Nathan chat to Arthur as they'd come down the hall.

"I brought donuts." Nathan kicked off his sneakers and dropped the box on the island. In the living room, Ryn's eyes popped open, and she was on her feet with unnatural speed.

Deanna went to grab plates, but by the time she turned back each werewolf had a donut in their hands—and in Cole's case, halfway down his throat. Jamie reached for a plate, and Kiara swallowed her bite of rainbow sprinkle and dropped the donut on the plate Deanna offered.

"You guys are lucky I'm not trying to poison you," Nathan observed. He chose the double chocolate.

"I'd smell poison." Ryn licked powdered sugar from her fingers. Kiara forced herself to look away and not think about how, if she kissed Ryn right now, Ryn would taste as sweet as the missing sugar.

"Okay, now that everyone is fed—"

Cole was already reaching for his second donut.

"—I think we should sit down and talk about what's going on and what we can do." Nathan retrieved his mug from the counter and gestured at the living room.

"I don't know anything more." Kiara decided it was best to bluntly head off any questions.

Nathan rolled his eyes. "I said sit down first."

Annoyed at herself for feeling chastised, Kiara took her mug and her donut and went into the living room. Ryn had resumed her seat on the couch, so Kiara sat in the armchair. Cole chose the large black beanbag, settling himself into it with every appearance of comfort, and Jamie and Deanna joined Ryn on the couch. Nathan answered the beeping microwave, pulled out his reheated cup of coffee, and folded himself on the area rug in front of the coffee table.

"So," he said finally. "We don't know anything more, but now that we're all relatively sober and well-rested, I think it might be best if we go over what we do know." He pulled out a pen and notebook from the coffee table's lower shelf and twisted to look expectantly at Kiara.

"We were raised hearing about the Huntsmen. They're not supposed to be real, not exactly. They're like... the boogeyman. They'll get you if you're bad." Kiara shrugged and looked helplessly at Cole. She didn't know how to explain the sudden collision of their lives with what amounted to a fairy tale.

"You told me you thought they were real." Ryn leaned forward and caught Kiara's eyes. "You said no one talked about it, not really, but that you thought they were real. You warned me to be careful."

Kiara looked away, uncomfortable suddenly in the comfortable armchair. She remembered the conversation Ryn was talking about: curled under the sheets in the small room Ryn rented, with snow blowing heavily against the windows and lit candles placed throughout the room. Kiara had wanted them to never leave.

"I wanted you to know about them." Kiara was the first other werewolf Ryn had ever met, and Ryn's complete lack of knowledge about their world had been troubling—terrifying, actually.

"There are enough stories about them that it's not an unreasonable conclusion." Cole shrugged. "Our pack hasn't had dealings with them, but I think others have. It's not spoken about. We're supposed to police ourselves, you understand. According to tradition, the Huntsmen are what happens if we can't, or won't. It's embarrassing for a pack to be unable to control their members or deal with their own problems. Embarrassing for GNAAW as well. But occasionally packs try to hide things from GNAAW. Not everyone is content to be supervised and regulated." He gave a wry grin at Ryn. "When they try to deal with problems on their own, when what they need is support, things can go wrong. And that's when the Huntsmen supposedly come in."

"Okay, hang on." Deanna set her mug on the coffee table with a clatter. Anger colored her cheeks. "Where the hell were these guys last year? Where were they when crywolf wouldn't leave me alone, when he showed up at the *Wolf's Run* event? If these guys are so worried about keeping everyone safe, where were they then?" Her voice broke on the last word and with a furious sob she turned to Jamie, who wrapped her up and held her close. Over the top of Deanna's head, Jamie met Kiara's hard eyes with her own.

"It's a good question, K."

"It is. And I don't know. This isn't something we—" Kiara gestured to herself and Cole. "Have any experience with."

"And Uncle Michael?" Jamie asked.

"I don't know." Kiara was getting tired of repeating it. "Dad's never said anything about them beyond the boogeymen stuff."

"Again—" Nathan broke in. "I think we need to stop talking about what we don't know, and talk about what we do. So," he read back to them. "The Huntsmen are a human policing force. They know about werewolves. They are after one, or all, of the werewolves in this room. Is that correct?"

Kiara nodded.

"We don't know how they know about us, we don't know what they know about us, and we're not sure what it is, exactly, that they want." Nathan tapped his pen against the table. "Can one of you who was there last night run me through what happened? In *detail*," he stressed.

"We spotted them in the club. The axe is supposed to be their symbol, and there were at least two of them in the bar with axe tattoos. When we got out onto the street, there was another. Three in total. One woman, two men. They cornered us, drew weapons, and threatened Deanna." Kiara paused, reluctant to describe what happened after that.

"Kiara stopped the one pointing the gun at me," Deanna broke in. "The other two ran. And then we left."

"And you're pretty sure they didn't follow you here?"

Kiara nodded. "Fairly sure."

"All right." Nathan set down his pen and chewed on his lip. "We called your dad—your Alpha—he said he'd talk to GNAAW, and now we're here."

"We are," Cole agreed. "And I think the best thing we can do is wait. Dad will get back to us today, probably. But until we know more, I think what Kiara said last night is still our best option—we stay here."

"The werewolves at least, yeah." Nathan nodded. "From what you've told me, I don't think the Huntsmen would hurt a human. After all, their whole thing is to, like, protect us from you. So Deanna and I can probably come and go as we please."

"Deanna was with us at the club," Jamie pointed out. "They had no problem holding her at gunpoint. I don't know if it's safe for her to leave. Not when they know she knows us."

Nathan rubbed at his eyebrows. "Okay, so I can leave. Probably. Because we're hoping they don't know we are here. Does anyone need anything?" he offered.

"My bike," Ryn said, at the same time as Deanna said "My computer."

Nathan nodded at Deanna, then switched his focus to Ryn. "Where's your bike?"

"It was outside the club, locked up. If it's still there."

Nathan nodded. "Got it. Okay. Here's what we are going to do. I'm going to shower, get dressed, and go grab Deanna's computer and Ryn's bike. I'll also buy groceries, because I don't have enough food in the house for this many people."

"Sugar," Kiara put in.

Nathan shot her a glance. "While I'm in the shower, you can make a list of whatever you want or might need. I'll only be a couple hours, max, and maybe we'll have heard from your dad when I get back. Sound good?"

Everyone nodded.

"Great." Nathan went into the bathroom. Deanna picked up his notebook and ripped out a page to begin making a grocery list.

"Sugar," Kiara said again, unnecessarily, judging from Deanna's eye roll.

Deanna passed the list to Ryn, who jotted something on the bottom and then held it out for Kiara. Kiara took it and decided she had nothing else to add—Deanna had written "SUGAR" in all caps across the top half of the page—so passed it to Cole.

"All right, kids," Cole said, glancing at the list. "What do you want to do today?"

RYN'S BIKE WAS PARKED HAPHAZARDLY in the front hallway, and Kiara scowled at it as she walked out of the bathroom. Though Nathan's apartment wasn't tiny, having six people and one dog in a space with walls or doors only for the bathroom, made privacy impossible. It hadn't been twenty-four hours, but already Kiara was ready to jump out of her skin.

The apartment was a bit like Vancouver itself, Kiara thought ruefully. Even in the two-bedroom apartment she shared with Cole in the neighboring Olympic Village, they were one unit in a building of hundreds. No matter where you went in the city, people were everywhere. Kiara longed for the solitude of her parents' acreage and the quiet woods that surrounded them.

In the kitchen, Jamie and Nathan bickered good-naturedly over what to make for dinner. Deanna and Ryn were on the couch with controllers clutched in their hands as they played *Borderlands* on Nathan's PS4.

No one looked up as Kiara reentered the main room, and Kiara kept her head down to avoid eye contact as she went to the stairs.

Cole sat on Nathan's bed, propped up with pillows against the headboard, and read a paperback. Kiara sank beside him, and he lifted an arm so she could snuggle in. "*The Lord of the Fading Lands?*" She asked skeptically, reading the cover of what could only be a lurid paranormal romance with a snarling larger-than-life black cat and a "mystical" looking male cover model on the front.

"It's not that bad." Cole closed the book, and on the back Kiara caught a glimpse of what was presumably the same cat, but wearing wings and breathing fire.

"Did you bring that with you?"

"No." Cole gestured at the bookcase that took up the far wall of Nathan's bedroom. "I thought it looked interesting."

"You have the weirdest taste."

Cole just smiled, pulled her close, and rested his chin on the top of her head. "How are you doing?"

Though she doubted anyone downstairs could hear her—Ryn and Jamie could probably tell that the two of them were talking, but unless they focused wouldn't be able to make out their words—Kiara lowered her voice before she answered. "I'm okay. It's... I never thought I'd see her again."

"And now that you have?"

Kiara shrugged against his side, unwilling, unable, to answer. Untangling her emotions about Ryn had always been an impossible task, one that hadn't gotten easier with time.

"I wish it wasn't like this," Kiara responded finally. She wished she wasn't seeing Ryn when everything was a mess, when Kiara had absolutely no idea how to get them out of it or why they were in it in the first place.

Cole stroked his sister's arm. Kiara allowed herself to relax fully into his side, and Cole shifted slightly so that he could resume reading his book. Kiara let her eyes slide shut. She'd never been much for naps, hated them, in fact, but her lack of sleep from the night before was catching up with her and she could feel herself beginning to doze off.

Abruptly, she was yanked out of it. Something had cut through the noise, and everyone ceased talking at the same time. Downstairs, a phone buzzed against the counter for a second time.

Kiara scrambled off the bed and down the stairs; Cole moved with slightly more dignity on her heels. Jamie met her at the bottom and handed Kiara her phone. There were two texts from Dad, and Kiara hastily unlocked the phone and pulled them up.

Have a call with GNAAW rep tonight.

Stay put. Will call you after.

Kiara read them out loud and tried not to grit her teeth. The tension in the room deflated.

"So we keep doing nothing." Ryn tossed her controller to the couch beside her with more force than necessary. "I can't lose another day of work, or reschedule another set of appointments. I'm going to lose clients I can't afford."

"I know," Kiara replied wearily. "I'm sorry."

"Sorry doesn't pay my rent." Ryn stalked out the living room. Kiara's hand shot out and caught her arm as she passed.

"You can't leave," Kiara reminded her, hating herself for doing it when Ryn sent her a withering glare and yanked her arm free.

"Yeah. I got that. I'm going to the roof for some air. Unless that's not allowed either?" She arched a mocking eyebrow.

"No, that's fine." Kiara stepped back, the fleeting heat of Ryn's skin still warm against her palm.

Nathan turned to the kitchen and busied himself grating ginger.

"Dinner will be in thirty minutes," he called after Ryn. She raised her hand in a salute and slammed the front door behind her.

"Do you think one of us should maybe go after her?" Deanna gnawed on her bottom lip. "She forgot her shoes. And, I mean, I know how frustrating it can be to get thrown into all this pack stuff…"

"Sure. Whatever," Kiara said. "If you want to get your head bit off, be my guest."

Deanna exchanged a cautious side-eye with Jamie and went to the door, where she scooped up both her flats and Ryn's oxfords.

Once the door had closed for the second time, Kiara slumped on the couch and put her head in her hands. Cole went to help Nathan in the kitchen and tied the extra apron around his waist. Beside Kiara the couch shifted as Jamie sat.

"This better not be another heart to heart," Kiara warned, not lifting her head.

"Yeah, no. We've all had enough of that." Jamie shoved Deanna's neglected controller into Kiara's lap and picked up Ryn's abandoned one. "Let's play."

Chapter Ten |

KIARA DIDN'T SLEEP ANY BETTER the second night, and was up at six to call her father. Actually, she'd woken up at four-thirty, but had waited an hour and a half until she figured he'd be up. She wasn't sure why he hadn't called her back last night, and her multiple texts and then calls—both to his cell and the house—had gone unanswered. Cole had urged her not to worry, but the line between his eyes had betrayed his own concern.

Kiara stepped out into the hallway and eased the door shut behind her, not wanting to wake up the other members of the pack or Ryn. She called home.

"Kiara." Her father answered on the second ring; his voice was hoarser than usual. "I'm sorry I didn't call you. After our meeting it was late—well, early, really—and I wanted to let you get some sleep."

"I didn't," Kiara responded shortly. "What happened?"

"It's good news, sort of." A door clicked shut on his end of the line, and Kiara suspected that he'd stepped outside, too. "It's not you they're after. Not our pack."

"So we're safe." Relief left Kiara weak, and she sagged against the far wall of the hallway. She could go back home, *Ryn* could go back home, and everything could go back to normal, normal meaning without Ryn. Which, Kiara reminded herself, was good. "Hang on—so GNAAW knows about the Huntsmen? And not only knows about them, but is in contact with them?"

"Yes." Her father's voice was weary. "Apparently there's a line of communication between the two, for situations such as this."

"Why didn't we know about that?"

"I asked the same question. Apparently it's bad publicity—GNAAW wants its members to trust the Assembly. Confirming the existence of the Huntsmen would raise too many questions about GNAAW's ability to police itself."

"It doesn't really matter, I guess. Now that we're done with them." The relief of it was immense.

"They want Taryn Lee."

Kiara flew off the wall. "What? Why? She hasn't done anything."

"Apparently the incident last year with Jamie wasn't kept as quiet as GNAAW had hoped. Their man says the Huntsmen caught wind, and now they're going after any lone wolves. They think that's what caused crywolf to go rogue. They're insisting that any wolf without a pack is unsafe, a danger."

"Ryn—Taryn—isn't a danger. She's never hurt anyone. She wouldn't."

"I believe that. But this isn't something we can decide. GNAAW has offered to protect her—"

"She won't accept." Kiara shook her head.

"That's between her and GNAAW. But this is good news. This means you don't have to stay in hiding anymore."

"And R—Taryn? She's just supposed to, what, go out and hope she doesn't run into the Huntsmen? How does GNAAW even contact them? And how did they know about Ryn in the first place? She's not exactly involved in werewolf society."

"I don't know. The GNAAW representative, Davis, wasn't sure about that either."

"And he's not concerned? Ryn's a werewolf. She's one of us. Shouldn't GNAAW want to keep *all of us* safe?"

"He says—"

"And what are they going to do with her if they find her? They attacked us two nights ago. Attacked us, Dad. One of them had a *gun*, with who knows what kind of bullets. Am I supposed to just let Ryn get killed because she's by herself?"

"No, Kiara, of course not. We're not 'letting' anyone get killed."

"It sounds like that's what you're suggesting."

"I'm not." Her father's voice was curt. "You know I wouldn't condone that. But this is a whole hell of a lot bigger than us. The Huntsmen are—"

"Apparently in charge of us now." Kiara was too furious to stand still and paced down the long hallway with her bare feet slapping against the concrete. "I can't believe you're just backing down like this."

"I'm not backing down," her father snapped. "I'm protecting our pack. Which is what you should be doing. Mr. Davis will be reaching out to you today, and I expect you to treat him with far more respect than you're currently showing me."

"Right, because that's a two-way road."

"Kiara, you will do what's best for our pack. Our priority, first and foremost, is *always* to keep our family safe. If you have problems with how GNAAW is run, we can discuss that after this current situation has been dealt with. But right now is no time for your stubborn—"

"It sounds like we could use a little more 'stubborn,' Dad, considering you were willing to just roll over and give up Ryn without—"

"Watch your tone." There was a low warning growl in her father's voice, his wolf leaking through his normally ironclad control.

"Yes, sir, Alpha, sir." Kiara mocked a salute with her middle finger. "Thanks for the call. You've been really helpful." She hung up before he could respond.

She got to the end of the hallway and dropped her forehead against the cool metal of the fire door to the stairs. Exhaustion weighed heavily on her shoulders, and she wanted nothing more than to crawl into bed—her own bed—and sleep for twelve hours. Unfortunately, she couldn't say when she'd have that chance again. There was no world in which she would leave Ryn to face the Huntsmen, and maybe GNAAW, alone. She would have to tell the others what her father had said. He was their Alpha, and Jamie and Cole would be duty-bound to listen to him. Kiara could see the logic if they did. Ryn was nothing to them except a problem, which is all she should be to Kiara.

Lifting her head from the door, Kiara turned around and squared her shoulders.

"WHAT DID HE SAY?"

Too busy rehearsing what *she* was going to say, Kiara wasn't prepared for Ryn to be waiting just inside Nathan's doorway.

"Jesus." Kiara pressed a hand to her chest to still her startled heart and scowled. "Give me some space."

"I didn't catch all of it, but I caught enough." Ryn stepped back, but was clearly unwilling to wait. "What did your dad say? What did GNAAW say?"

Kiara pushed past her. "I'll tell you when everyone is up. We can all—"

"No." Ryn followed Kiara into the kitchen. "No," she repeated. "I heard my name. I didn't hear what your dad said, but I heard what *you* said. I know it's about me. That's who they're after, isn't it?" She ran a frustrated hand through her long hair. "Your perfect little pack is playing by all the rules, but not me." Her smile was defiant, but it couldn't completely mask the vulnerability beneath. "And now you're caught up in my mess again."

"It's not like that."

"It's always been like that."

"Taryn—"

"Don't worry. I'll get out of your hair. This obviously isn't your problem." Ryn was already moving out of the kitchen. "I'll get my stuff and go."

"Stop it. You're not going anywhere. I'm not just going to let you—"

"You don't get to let me do anything." Ryn started to make her way up the stairs but was stopped by a sleepy but cheerful Deanna, who was attempting to twist her bedhead into a bun.

"Good morning!" Deanna kept coming down the stairs, forcing Ryn back. "It's probably too early to start arguing, since none of us have had coffee. Let's have coffee first and then we can argue."

"We're not arguing," Ryn began. "I'm leaving, and that's the end of it."

"Oh, come on." Now it was Jamie's turn to block Ryn's access up the stairs. "You can't go without breakfast. Cole is going to make French toast and he makes really good French toast. It's like the only thing he can make."

"I can make other stuff," Cole objected from upstairs.

Jamie shook her head. "He can't," she mouthed.

"This is all very sweet, but I'm serious." Ryn attempted the stairs a third time, but Nathan stumbled halfway down and sat.

"Someone bring me coffee," he mumbled, squinting as he cleaned his glasses on his T-shirt. "Cole is a cuddler, did anyone know that? He cuddles. All night. It's suffocating. I don't think I slept for more than five minutes at a time."

"You cuddled right back." Cole ruffled Nathan's hair fondly on his way down. Nathan made a disgusted noise and tried to squirm out of the way.

"I didn't!" Nathan protested. "If anything, I was trying to get away from you."

"Guys!" Ryn shouted. "This isn't a joke! I'm the one they're after, so I'm going to leave."

"I feel like we've done this before. Haven't we done this before?" Nathan tossed the question to Jamie.

"We have done this before," Jamie agreed. "It's becoming a pattern."

"Okay, that was a bit different," Deanna argued. "I mean, I left, but not to deal with it on my own. I left you to deal with it. Sorry," she added with a guilty wince at Jamie.

"It's fine; if anything, that made more sense than what Ryn is trying to do." Jamie gave Deanna a kiss on the cheek as she started making coffee.

"For fuck's sake," Ryn growled. "What are you talking about?"

"Last year someone was after Deanna. Just Deanna," Nathan began.

"All the other *Wolf's Run* players too," Deanna corrected.

"Right, but, like, out of *us* it was just Deanna. And did we send Deanna off on her own to deal with the horrible rogue werewolf? No, we did not. We—well, Jamie—called in the cavalry." Nathan gestured theatrically at Cole and Kiara.

"Because it was ludicrous for you to try and stop him by yourself." Kiara crossed her arms over her chest.

"Totally agreed," Nathan said cheerfully. "Completely idiotic to think we could do it on our own."

Ryn rolled her eyes. "This is a bit different."

"It's not." Deanna shook her head. "Not really. Let us help, Ryn."

"How are you going to help?"

"We've got a place for you to stay, for starters." Nathan came down the stairs. "I get what it's like to feel like you have to do everything on your own. I do," he said quietly. "But sometimes you have to let other people help. And that's okay too."

Ryn gave a jerky, defensive shrug.

"We know how GNAAW works. We understand the system." Cole started to pull the ingredients for French toast from the fridge. "Give us a bit more time."

"Today." Kiara held Ryn's gaze. "They'll get in touch with us today. Stay until then." Once they heard from GNAAW, they could reevaluate. Once they knew more, Kiara would know what to do. Until then, all she could do was keep Ryn here, where she knew she was safe. "Please."

Ryn's jaw worked; clearly stubbornness was warring with common sense. Kiara's shoulders tensed and her muscles knotted as she waited for Ryn to decide. If Ryn disagreed, Kiara didn't know what she would do. She couldn't keep Ryn in the apartment without a fight and, while Kiara was fairly confident that she could win, she wasn't sure what winning that fight would make her lose.

"Sure. Whatever." Ryn dropped onto the couch and pulled out her phone to demonstrate her clear indifference.

"Great." Deanna beamed. "This means you can do my hair and Jamie's!"

"What?" Jamie looked startled and raised a self-conscious hand to her hair. "What's wrong with it?"

"You know how we were talking about how you needed a trim the other day," Deanna reminded Jamie.

"Oh. Er. Right. A trim."

"And Nathan probably needs one too, right?" Deanna turned her smile, sharp at the edges, to Nathan.

"Yeah. Definitely. It's out of control." Nathan feigned concern.

"What about you, Kiara?" Ryn looked up from her screen. Her voice was syrupy-sweet and set Kiara's teeth on edge. "You've definitely been seeing someone subpar."

Kiara didn't bother to dignify that with a response. "I'll take Arthur out," she offered and reached for the leash.

"Nope." Jamie pushed her hand away. "They saw you, us—" She indicated herself and Deanna. "—leave the Kings of Hearts with Ryn. If they're looking for her, then they're probably keeping their eyes out for us. So it's gotta be Nathan or Cole."

Cole shrugged innocently. "I'm cooking."

With a reluctant glance at the rainy windows, Nathan picked up the leash.

"Come on, buddy," he waved Arthur over, who gave a happy woof. "Out into the wilderness."

"Thaaank you," Deanna called after him as she settled onto one of the island stools.

"Is there a gym in the building?" Kiara asked Deanna. She itched with the need to get out of the apartment, to do something with the restless energy that burned under the surface of her skin.

"Yeah. You need a key, though."

Kiara deflated. *Of course.* And she was sure Nathan had left with it.

"There's one on my keychain. In my purse." Deanna jerked her thumb at the couch where her heart-shaped dancing purse sat on the floor beside the armrest—the one Ryn lounged against.

Kiara slid her eyes to Deanna and tilted her head hopefully in the direction of the couch. Deanna gave her a pitying look.

Kiara scowled.

Jamie turned her laugh into a hasty cough and busied herself in the kitchen with Cole.

Kiara gritted her teeth and crossed the room. Ryn didn't deign to look up from her phone, and Kiara tried not to be annoyed. She grabbed Deanna's purse, walked to the kitchen, and dug until she found the keys.

"Thanks." She slid the purse across the island. "I'll be back in a bit."

"Breakfast will be ready in twenty," Cole informed her.

Kiara waved a hand in acknowledgment and went to find the gym.

Chapter Eleven |

THE GYM WASN'T TOO HARD to find. Kiara just had to follow the smell of sweat, frustration, and endorphins to the second floor. This early on a Sunday morning, with most folks sleeping off their Saturday night, it was empty, which suited her well enough.

The bank of windows at the far wall gave her a slight pause, not that there was any way for the Huntsmen to know where they were. No, it was beyond paranoid to think that someone might be watching her through them. Still, Kiara wished the windows had curtains.

She realized she should have asked Nathan—or rather, Deanna, who obviously knew her way around Nathan's closets well enough—for another set of clothes, as the pair of baggy sweatpants and over-large T-shirt weren't ideal for working out, but there was no way Kiara was going back up. Besides, she reasoned, she could get a new set when she was finished, rather than dirty another outfit. And now that they knew the Huntsmen weren't after anyone in her pack, she might be able to get to her apartment for her own clothes. Or at least send Nathan.

Thinking fondly about the look of exasperation he'd give her when she asked him to go, Kiara went straight to the bench and loaded plates onto the bar.

KIARA WAS WINDING DOWN WHEN the lock on the gym door clicked and Nathan pushed his way through. He held a bottle of water and an aromatic plate of food. As he crossed the floor, he tossed her the bottle, and she caught it with a grateful nod.

Wiping sweat from her upper lip, Kiara twisted the cap off the bottle and sucked back half the water in one swallow.

"Thanks," she panted.

"No problem." Nathan watched as Kiara tidied away the evidence of her inhuman lifting ability.

"You didn't have to bring me breakfast." Kiara sat beside him and reached for a piece of French toast. She was ravenous enough not to care about the lack of utensils.

"What? Oh, this definitely isn't for you." Nathan jerked the plate out of her reach. Kiara's face fell, and he cackled. "Kidding, only kidding. God, you should have seen your face." He mimicked her expression, dropping his jaw in feigned dismay.

Kiara glowered and snatched the plate out of his grip before he could pull it away again. Neither she nor Cole were adept at cooking, but Cole was able to make a pretty good slice of French toast.

"I appreciate what you're doing for us," Kiara said after she'd inhaled the first piece.

Nathan raised an eyebrow. "All I did was bring you a plate of lukewarm, soggy bread."

Kiara gave him a flat look. "You know what I mean. Letting us stay at your place, getting involved in werewolf politics that have nothing to do with you. I appreciate it. We appreciate it," she added, stiffly. "Once this is over, I'll compensate you for the trouble."

Nathan stood abruptly, forcing Kiara to tilt her head to look up at him as she bit into her second piece. His hands were clenched at his sides, and he refused to look at her. When he spoke, his voice was terse. "You don't have to 'compensate' me for shit. And, frankly, I'm insulted at the offer."

Kiara swallowed the bite of toast that had suddenly become a lump in her throat. "You're not involved in this," she tried to explain. "It doesn't concern you. You're human."

"Yeah? Well so is Deanna, and that didn't stop her from getting caught in the crosshairs. Literally." Nathan paced away in disgust. "Deanna, Jamie, Cole, and even *you*—you're my friends. Assuming that I could, that I would, just turn my back on all of you is—is—"

"Unfair," Kiara realized. "I'm sorry. I didn't mean to imply—"

"Well, you did." Nathan turned back, stiffly, but with indignation fading.

"I won't again. But—"

Nathan sent her a sharp look.

"But," Kiara continued, "Let me at least reimburse you for the grocery bill for the weekend. We are eating an awful lot of your food." She held up the plate to demonstrate. "And it's not like I can't afford it."

"All right," Nathan allowed. "Are you finished with your workout?"

Kiara nodded and shoved the rest of the French toast in her mouth. She stood and wiped her icing sugar fingers on her T-shirt, figuring she'd be taking it off soon.

"Come on then." Nathan headed toward the door. "There's more French toast upstairs, and syrup."

IN NATHAN'S APARTMENT, RYN HAD set up an unconventional hair station on the far side of the kitchen island. In lieu of a mirror, Deanna—who was good at that sort of thing—had set up Nathan's large desktop Mac and turned on the webcam.

Jamie fidgeted self-consciously on the barstool as Ryn pulled her kit from her duffel bag. Ryn ignored Kiara's entrance and laid out her tools on the island.

"Stop freaking out," she said to Jamie. "I'm not going to do anything drastic. You'll look amazing, I promise."

"I'm not nervous," Jamie insisted, despite the fact that every werewolf in the room could smell the spike in her anxiety.

Ryn laughed.

Though Kiara was sticky with sweat and icing sugar, she decided a shower could wait. Nathan had promised her syrup with her next round, after all.

"Leftovers are just in the fridge," Cole called to Kiara from the living room. He sat on the couch reading the same book as last night, with Arthur draped adoringly over his lap—Nathan hadn't been wrong earlier, Cole would cuddle with anyone. Deanna was sunk into the beanbag with her laptop balanced on her lap and hummed a Taylor Swift song as she worked.

"All right, so." Ryn finished laying out her tools and stepped behind Jamie. She ran her hands though Jamie's short hair, and Jamie gave a full-body shiver in response.

Ryn's eyes lit with mischievous delight, and she ran her fingers through Jamie's hair. Jamie squirmed; a blush rose to her cheeks.

Kiara slammed the door on the microwave.

"Don't worry, love, some folks just like the sensation. Relax. Enjoy it." Ryn leaned down until her lips were an inch from Jamie's ear. Across the island, her dark eyes met Kiara's. "I promise to take *very* good care of you."

Jamie's blush deepened, the tips of her ears flushed red, and from her beanbag an amused snort interrupted Deanna's humming.

"Can you take care of me next?" Nathan had sidled up beside Kiara and, batting his eyelashes, leaned suggestively across the island toward Ryn.

Kiara elbowed him in the ribs.

"Ow." He straightened to rub the spot where her elbow had dug in. "Just for that I'm not going to show you where the syrup is."

"Fridge door," Cole commented from the couch, without looking up from his book. Nathan made a wounded sound of betrayal.

By the time Kiara had wolfed down her second plate of breakfast and showered, it was Deanna's turn for a haircut, and she hopped eagerly into the chair.

Jamie and Nathan had joined Cole in the living room. They were taking what Kiara was sure would be a zillion selfies of their new haircuts. Jamie's pompadour had been given a cleanup; the top was a little shorter so her waves were more pronounced. Ryn had done something more exciting with Nathan's hair. He sported elaborate edging on both sides of his head, in a floral pattern that thoroughly impressed Kiara, although she'd never admit it.

"I want to look a bit gayer, you know?" Deanna fussed with her hair in the computer-cum-mirror. "But I also don't want to go super short or anything because I like having long hair. It's just frustrating being so femme sometimes, because I know the hot queer girls I check out just think I'm gawking."

Kiara glanced at Jamie, wondering what she thought about Deanna checking out other girls, but her cousin seemed unconcerned as she continued to mug for Nathan's phone camera.

"I get you." Ryn nodded behind Deanna. "If I had access to all of my color, we'd add some fashion colors—non-natural color," she clarified. "You're already blonde, so we could do pretty much anything... you'd look amazing with an icy blue ombre. We call it denim," she added with a flashing smile.

"But I think I can come up with something acceptably queer—without getting rid of these lovely curls." She twined one around her finger and smiled, meeting Deanna's eyes in the screen.

Kiara wasn't sure what to do with the jealousy that simmered in her stomach as she witnessed the ease with which Deanna befriended Ryn. Kiara remembered all too well how banter with Ryn felt, remembered the high when Ryn met her eyes over a shared laugh. How easily the high could turn to heat with a quirk of Ryn's eyebrow or a curl of Kiara's lip.

The edgy, restless feeling hit again, and for the thousandth time Kiara checked her phone. It was fully charged, connected to Nathan's Wi-Fi and her service provider, and there'd been no contact from anyone.

She marveled if the fact that she wasn't fending off worried texts from friends wondering where she was, or what was the reason for her radio silence, but everyone in Vancouver that Kiara cared about was in this room. This was her family. She didn't need any other friends.

Well, not none, she considered, eyeing Nathan as he howled with laughter over a particularly silly face Jamie had made. Though the argument could be made—and Kiara may very well have made it herself in the past—that Nathan was as good as a brother to Deanna, so he was family. Kiara ignored that. She had a friend.

"Hey." She interrupted Jamie's next attempt at making a face. "Quit goofing around."

Jamie looked up at her with a wounded expression. Nathan just looked annoyed.

"I want to play Smash Brothers. And I'd rather play with you two six-year-olds than the computer." Kiara stepped around them and dropped onto the couch. Arthur's tail gave a furious wag, and he wriggled around to throw himself in her lap—in the process driving a paw into Cole's groin with enough force that her impossible-to-ruffle bother swore aloud.

Jamie and Nathan glanced at each other. Nathan shrugged, tucked his phone in his pocket, and passed out the controllers.

"CHECK OUT MY UNDERCUT," DEANNA boasted. She turned around and lifted up her hair to display the closely shaved triangle on the back of her head. She twisted so that she could look at it in the monitor.

Nathan paused the game so they could all look. When Deanna let her hair fall it completely hid the shave; she could be as femme-presenting as she wanted, or show it off by twisting her hair up. Before Kiara could think better of it, she lifted a hand to her own hair, fingering the blunt edges of her bob.

"I love it," Jamie proclaimed. She rose from the couch and swept a giggling Deanna up in her arms.

Leaning against the island with her arms folded comfortably across her chest, Ryn watched them with apparent fondness and enough familiarity that Kiara frowned. Ryn hadn't met either woman until the night before last. But Ryn's eyes were soft, and her lips were curved upward in a gentle smile.

Kiara pulled her gaze away and sank against the couch, letting the pillows engulf her. She remembered seeing that look on Ryn's face, the same look of happiness for someone who wasn't herself. When they were together, Ryn had pressed Kiara about her large family with the curiosity of someone who had a small one. Kiara had found it easy to talk to Ryn about them.

Ryn had particularly enjoyed stories about Cole and Kiara and Jamie growing up together. They had other cousins, firsts and seconds and thirds—the very nature of a werewolf pack living in a human society meant that they stayed close—but Jamie was the one closest in age and location to Cole and Kiara.

Before Deanna, Jamie had never had a serious girlfriend. She'd dated a few women casually and had nursed a yearlong crush on a sociology prof, only to have her heart bruised, though not broken, when the professor gently rebuffed her flirting.

During the year Kiara and Ryn were together, when Kiara was so wrapped up in Ryn—around Ryn—that she'd nearly flunked out, too in love to see anything past Ryn, too busy lounging naked and blissed out in Ryn's bed to go to class, Kiara had confessed that she worried Jamie would never find such happiness. Jamie was shy, awkward, and horribly tongue-tied around cute girls. Kiara had worried to Ryn that no one would be able to see past Jamie's shyness, which was so easily interpreted as aloofness.

"She's wonderful. She's so good, so honestly good. What if no one ever sees that, Ryn? What if Jamie's always hidden, and no one loves her?"

Ryn had laughed and pulled Kiara in for a kiss. "That won't happen. Someone will see. And then *you'll* see that you were silly to worry. Silly, but sweet." Ryn kissed her again and again, and then Kiara stopped thinking about Jamie altogether.

Suddenly it was all too much for Kiara. She couldn't stay in Nathan's living room, staring at that open, fearless love, not when the only person she'd ever felt that with was in the same room, and between them was a chasm eight miles wide.

"I'm going for a smoke." Kiara pulled herself up from the couch and grabbed her phone and her purse. Ryn dug her hand into the pocket of the jeans she'd borrowed from Nathan and held out her lighter. Brushing past, Kiara refused to notice. She'd found an old book of matches in Nathan's kitchen drawer last night, amid the takeout menus and accumulated kitchen gadgets. She didn't need anything from Ryn.

Kiara took Cole's battered leather jacket from the hook by the door, slung it around her shoulders, and closed the front door firmly behind her.

Chapter Twelve |

It had finally stopped raining, but dampness hung in the February air. Kiara had never thought that she would miss the dry cold of an Edmonton winter—the chapped hands, chapped lips—but here everything was wet, and heavy with rain.

Kiara flicked open the lid on the carton, pulled out one of the slim cigarettes, and held it between her lips as she fumbled with the matches.

They were shit quality, but finally one caught and Kiara drew in the first lungful of smoke gratefully.

The roof looked different in the daylight. The view was less magical. Though downtown still rose, gleaming, not too far away, Nathan's neighborhood was in transition. New construction went on at every corner, and yet squat and ugly warehouses were still scattered throughout. Kiara walked to the opposite side of the roof and leaned her forearms against the ledge. Night hid the truth behind all the glowing lights—the sheer press of people that necessitated so many high-rises packed so close together. In the daylight it wasn't romantic; it was claustrophobic.

Kiara sighed. She could appreciate what other people—Jamie, Cole—saw in the city. It was a constant hub of activity, a place for art and leisure and with easy access to both coast and mountain. If the people weren't exactly friendly, they weren't deliberately rude either, and given the size of the place it wasn't too hard to find a niche.

Then again, it had never been places that drew Kiara, but people. Even before Kiara and Cole had hurried out the year before to answer Jamie's call for help, Cole had been talking about joining Jamie on the West Coast. The rescue-mission-cum-hasty-visit had cemented his decision, and if both Jamie and Cole were in Vancouver, Kiara could hardly stay behind.

Kiara stubbed the cigarette out on the ledge. There was no use analyzing herself, or the city, to death. She didn't have Ryn's urge to question everything, to ask *why*, and *who*, and *how*.

Though perhaps, she thought in a ludicrous moment of amusement, if she had they might know somewhat more about why the Huntsmen were after them, who they were, and how they'd been found out.

Kiara zipped Cole's coat closed against the chill of the wind that had picked up and pulled a second cigarette from the package. She'd take as much quiet time up here as she could.

And, as though the universe felt compelled to let her know that she'd never have an uninterrupted moment of solitude again, Kiara's phone rang.

Cigarette tucked between her fingers, she fumbled the phone out of her bag and swiped to answer the unfamiliar number requesting a video call.

A man's face filled the screen: mid-fifties, white, with graying hair and a pair of pale blue eyes. Kiara raised the phone so that he could see her, and he blinked. Unimpressed, she stared at him and waited for him to speak.

He cleared his throat. "Hello there, miss. I'm sorry, I think I might have the wrong number. Is this…" He looked down and rattled off Kiara's phone number.

"Yes."

"Ah." He frowned. "Michael Lyons gave me this number. I'm looking to speak to his heir." He glanced down again, and shuffled through paper. "My file tells me that Lyons' eldest child, his son, is Cole Lyons."

"That's correct."

His gaze shifted past Kiara as though looking for someone behind her. "Would you be a dear and pass him the phone? I really must speak to him."

"No."

His eyes sharpened and turned back to her. "Excuse me?"

"No," Kiara repeated, allowing herself a moment of satisfaction as the man—who was presumably the GNAAW rep—clenched his jaw.

"I'm calling on an important matter, young lady, and this isn't time to play games. I need to speak to Lyons' heir, and if you don't—"

"You are."

The man forced a chuckle. "Indeed. Well, if you would connect me with Cole Lyons directly—"

"Does your file give you the name of Michael Lyons' heir?"

"No." The rep's replies were getting shorter, his voice snappish. "But as his eldest, and in fact *only*, male child—"

"Last I checked, inheriting an Alpha's rank had little to do with sex assigned at birth, or birth order, for that matter, and everything to do with power. So if you'd like to speak to my brother, you're welcome to. But if you'd like to speak to Michael Lyons' heir, you are. And I'd suggest you avoid any further 'young lady's,' or 'dears.'"

"I—well—" the man sputtered. It only took him a moment to regain himself, but when he did his blue eyes were cooler. "You're Kiara Lyons then, Michael's second-born."

"And his only female child." Apparently that mattered in this conversation.

"My apologies." Kiara didn't miss the way his apologies neglected to include the words "I'm sorry." The man's voice smoothed out, and he stretched his lips in a smile that didn't meet his eyes. "I'm Ethan Davis."

Kiara waited.

Irritation flickered over Davis' face. "You and two other members of your pack were involved in an altercation with the Huntsmen two days ago."

"If you could call being stalked, threatened, and having a gun pulled on one of our members an 'altercation,' then yes," Kiara answered coolly.

His lips thinned at the interruption. "We received reports that one of the Huntsmen was rather severely injured. As you are no doubt aware," he continued, condescension creeping into his voice, "it is simply inexcusable for a human to come to harm at the hands of a wolf."

He waited, as though expecting Kiara to respond. She didn't.

"Our reports further indicate that Taryn Nicole Lee was responsible for this injury. Now, had it been a member of your pack—a wolf therefore under GNAAW protection— we would of course deal with the matter internally, but as Taryn Nicole Lee is a lone wolf, GNAAW is unable to step in. We therefore ask that you cease harboring Taryn Nicole Lee and turn her over to the Huntsmen."

"Whoever is sending in your reports is not doing a very good job." Kiara let boredom creep into her voice, and, because she knew it would annoy him, inspected the chipped polish on one of her fingernails. "Taryn Nicole Lee was not responsible for any harm to any human. I'm the one who threw the asshole against the wall, *after* he pointed the gun at one of our members." She looked up, expecting surprise, but there was no indication on his face that Kiara's admission was news to him. Kiara's eyes narrowed.

"It's noble of you to protect your... friend." His lips were pinched; his discomfort was evident. "But my report was very clear that the perpetrator of the violence was, in fact, Taryn Nicole Lee. And there was no mention of any gun." His eyes hardened. "Twisting the facts in order to protect a wolf like Taryn does both of us a disservice."

"There's only one person twisting facts here." Questions raced through Kiara's head. Who had reported the confrontation in the alleyway to GNAAW, other than her father? Her father knew Kiara's version—the truth—and would have told GNAAW exactly that. Was

GNAAW in far closer contact with the Huntsmen than Kiara's pack was aware? Whose purpose did it serve to scapegoat Taryn? And even *if* it had been Taryn who had attacked the man with the gun, she would have done so only to protect Deanna. Surely protecting a human was equally as important as not harming one.

"Be careful with your accusations. This is a serious matter, and I don't have time for nonsense. I need you to agree that you will turn over Taryn Nicole Lee to the Huntsmen. I will then arrange a time and place for the handover, and we can consider this matter closed." Davis clicked a pen and noted something on the paper in front of him.

"No." Kiara shook her head. "No. No one is handing Taryn over to anyone. Who was responsible for this report? It's wildly inaccurate and I'm not going to fucking *turn over—*"

"Watch your language, young lady."

The anger that had been mounting through their entire conversation finally crested, and with it came a sudden, terrifying calm. "That's 'Alpha-designate Lyons,' Mr. Davis. As Alpha Lyons' heir *I* outrank *you,* and therefore you will speak to me with the respect I am owed or you will not speak to me at all. Is that clear?"

Davis looked up from his paper. His blue eyes simmered with banked rage, and he carefully set the pen down.

"*Is that clear?*"

"Yes, Alpha-designate Lyons." Any pretense at goodwill vanished.

"Good." Kiara kept her eyes steady and cool on his as she outlined her position. "I will not surrender Taryn Nicole Lee to the Huntsmen or to GNAAW. I will accept full responsibility for the injury done to the Huntsman, but I will not apologize for it to anyone, as it was an act of self-defense against someone who intended harm to my pack. The Huntsmen therefore can have no legitimate reason for wanting Taryn. I expect you to communicate these things to your superiors and to the Huntsmen, as you are apparently in contact with them. As the Huntsmen have no cause, however, I cannot fathom why they have GNAAW support and I suggest you have a word with whomever is providing you with inaccurate 'reports.'

"At this point I believe we can both consider the matter closed. Thank you for your call, Mr. Davis." Without waiting for a response, Kiara ended the call.

Outrage burned low in her gut, and Kiara dropped her phone into her purse before putting it on the ground beside her. She relit her cigarette with steady hands.

Kiara started to pace, trying to figure out the conversation she'd just had. GNAAW and the Huntsmen obviously had a far closer relationship than Kiara, or anyone in her pack, had been aware of. Davis' report could only have come from the Huntsmen. It made sense, almost. If GNAAW and the Huntsmen were both in the business of keeping werewolves out of the spotlight and hidden from the general human populace, they were bound to have worked together. So cooperation was to be expected, if downplayed.

What didn't line up, though, what set Kiara's teeth on edge, was the patently wrong detail that it had been Ryn, not her, who had injured the Huntsman with the gun, that, and the fact that presumably it had been Ryn they had been after. If Kiara and Jamie hadn't happened to be at Kings of Hearts the same night that Ryn was performing…

Kiara took a long drag from the cigarette, and when she pulled it away she noticed her fingers were trembling. If they hadn't been there, Ryn would have had no chance. It wasn't that Kiara didn't think Ryn could defend herself. Ryn had enough practice with that. After all, she was a loner and a lone wolf and a habitual breaker of norms. But she would have been outnumbered, at least three to one, and there was ample evidence that the Huntsmen hadn't wanted to simply have a *conversation* with her.

If that had happened, Ryn could have been dead. She would have been in the same city as Kiara, moving in roughly the same queer circles—in a city the size of Vancouver, there were only so many of them—and Kiara would never had known. Kiara was certain that the Huntsmen would have simply made Ryn disappear. She would never have seen Ryn again, and would have spent the rest of her life wondering what Ryn was doing, imagining her life without Kiara, and never knowing that that life had been cruelly cut short long ago.

Kiara's pacing was fast enough now that she kicked up the gravel from the roof with every step. Her heartbeat thundered in her ears. The cigarette was a long line of ash, and she was suddenly aware of the heat in the tips of her fingers that meant she was about to get burned. She dropped the butt and ground it out with the toe of her boot. She didn't know how many times she'd paced the length of the roof, but now she stood facing downtown again. The wind picked up, and Kiara raised a hand—fingers still unsteady—to the cold tracks of tears on her cheeks.

"Fuck," she muttered, rubbing at her eyes to destroy any trace of tears. "Fuck. Fuck, fuck, fuck!"

Chapter Thirteen |

TEN YEARS AGO...

"Hi, Kiara, it's your mom. I haven't heard from you in a while—is everything all right? Cole says you're dating someone; your dad and I would love to hear more about them! Anyway, give me a call back when you can. Hope school's going okay. Miss you!"

Kiara deleted the voicemail, only feeling a small twinge of guilt. She'd call her mom soon, but she didn't want to have to explain why she'd had to withdraw from one of her classes to avoid a failing grade.

"Everything okay at home?" Ryn lifted an enquiring eyebrow from where she stirred a pot of sauce on the stove.

"Yeah, it's fine." Kiara put her phone on silent and slid it across the table. "My mom just won't stop bugging me to call her."

"Didn't you just call her, like, last week?" Ryn asked.

"Yeah," Kiara shrugged self-consciously. "We usually talk every couple days, though."

Ryn gave an exaggerated shudder. "Ugh. Sounds suffocating."

"It's not that bad," Kiara said defensively.

"I can't imagine having to check in with someone." Ryn wrinkled her nose. "I mean, I guess if that's what you're used to…" Her tone implied incredulity that anyone could get used to such a thing.

Kiara picked at her nail polish. She'd never thought of it as checking in. She had a good relationship with her parents, with her brother. They didn't call to check in with one another, but to see how each other's lives were going. Or, at least, that's what she had always understood…

"You're right, though," she told Ryn. "I did just call her. I'll wait till next week."

Ryn nodded from the stove, and held up a wooden spoon covered in red sauce. "Come taste this and tell me if I need more salt."

☾

KIARA SPILLED OUT INTO THE night with Ryn's hand tucked securely in hers. The snow had stopped, finally, but the night was cold enough to steal Kiara's breath away. She tugged her coat tighter now that they were outside the smoky, sweaty club and wished she hadn't worn a skirt.

"We're never going to get a cab," Kiara moaned. "And the buses don't start again for another," she checked her phone, "Two hours."

"Aww, poor pack princess," Ryn teased. "Did it ever occur to you that there's another solution? One that doesn't require us to stand in the cold for two more hours."

Kiara furrowed her brow. "Do you know someone who can come pick us up?"

Ryn laughed delightedly. "Love, we don't need a ride. The night is ours—we're *made* for this."

"Ryn," Kiara said reluctantly. "We're not supposed to shift when someone might see us."

"Who's gonna see?" Ryn threw out her arms. "It's three in the morning, and it's colder than my Aunt Nari's side-eye. No one's gonna see us."

"We're in the middle of downtown."

"Come on," Ryn gave Kiara a gentle shove. "Live a little. Haven't you ever wondered what it would be like? To run through the city and know you own it? That no one can take that away from you?"

Kiara glanced at the street behind them. Now that they'd moved farther from the club, it was deserted in all directions. She'd lost track of how many shots she and Ryn had done in the club, but it was enough that alcohol buzzed through her system and awoke something wild and reckless.

"I've done it before," Ryn coaxed. "It was fine. No one saw me. And I got home in one piece, well before the sun rose and people started venturing out. It'll take us like, half an hour, max."

"Our clothes, though, my purse?" Kiara was wavering, and Ryn could tell.

"We'll stuff them there." Ryn pointed to a stack of milk cartons at the edge of a nearby alley. "And tomorrow we can come back for them."

"Well…" Kiara had a midterm tomorrow afternoon and she'd been planning to get up early to study since she'd missed the last few classes. *Not too early, though*, she thought, giggling, remembering that it was already tomorrow. "All right. As long as no one sees us."

Ryn grinned and grabbed Kiara so she could kiss her. Ryn tasted like alcohol, and warmth, and the menthol cigarettes Kiara had been smoking. Kiara's resolve crumbled, replaced with a mounting excitement. She had wondered what it would be like, but neither she nor her cousins had ever gotten up the nerve to disobey their parents and shift in a city.

Ryn let out an excited, drunken whoop and started to shed her clothing.

☾

"Where were you last night?" Kiara stood with her arms crossed in front of her chest, blocking Ryn's path out of the bathroom. "You didn't come home."

"Whoa, calm down there, buddy." Ryn gave a lopsided grin and slid past Kiara. "I was at Kyle's. We smoked a couple joints, I lost track of time. Whatever." She rummaged in the fridge and came out with a grimace and a half-full bottle of Gatorade. "There might have been a bottle of vodka in there, too." She laughed.

"Are you even sober right now?" Kiara demanded.

Ryn gestured at herself. "Do I look sober? I am grade A un-sober, love. You should try it some time."

"It's dangerous to get intoxicated around humans. You don't know what might happen if you lose control."

"See, that's your problem." Ryn crossed the room to jab a finger into the center of Kiara's chest. "You've got control issues coming out your ass. Just let go, love. Just let it go." She unscrewed the Gatorade and took a drink.

"Not all of us are so comfortable with irresponsibility," Kiara informed Ryn. "Some of us have enough respect for the others in our life that—"

"Save me the lecture." Ryn rolled her eyes. "If I want to hear what 'Alpha Lyons' has to say, I'll call up your dad."

"Fuck off."

"You fuck off. Shouldn't you be, like, in school or something anyway?" Ryn didn't wait for Kiara to answer, just stalked into her room and slammed the door.

☾

KIARA FUMBLED WITH HER KEYS and missed the lock twice before she managed to unlock the door. She dumped her book bag to the floor and tore at the scarf around her throat. Her fingers trembled, her breath came quick and short as her chest constricted. She couldn't get enough air. Her limbs were weak; she was dizzy and numb and her heartbeat pounded in her ears.

"Get off, get off." Her voice was high and hysterical behind her clenched teeth as she continued to yank at the scarf. If she could get the scarf off, she could breathe and she just needed to breathe—

"Kiara, love, hey." Ryn was there in an instant, her eyes wide. She grabbed Kiara's wrists and lifted them gently away from where they clawed at her throat.

"I need it off!"

"Here." Ryn's fingers were quick and deft, unwinding the scarf and helping Kiara out of her coat. "It's gone."

Kiara's panic didn't abate; her chest was tight and heaving. "Ryn."

"Tell me what's wrong." Ryn's hands rubbed soothingly over Kiara's arms.

Kiara jerked away, her gums itching as her body's fight-or-flight response warred with itself. "I failed Foundations of Mechatronics." She had known going into the final that she wasn't as prepared as she could have been. But she'd done the readings the night before. She only had to get a sixty on the final to get a passing grade.

Ryn laughed, and the response was like a bucket of cold water dumped on Kiara. "That it? Jesus, Kiara, I thought you'd killed someone." She picked up Kiara's bag and took it into the kitchen. Kiara followed.

"That's not *it*! You don't understand. Between this and the course I withdrew from—"

Ryn shrugged. "I don't know what you thought would happen. You've gone to what, half a dozen classes this semester? Maybe university just isn't your thing."

"It is, though." It was. It had been. Kiara had always gotten top grades. She'd never failed a course.

She glimpsed herself in the hallway mirror; her eyes had gone pale and gray. The pounding of her heartbeat was overwhelming—she could feel it, thick and urgent, in the hollow of her throat.

"Kiara, control yourself." Ryn's voice now had a sharp edge to it. "Sheena's in the next room."

Now that Ryn had drawn her attention, Kiara could just make out the sound of a third heartbeat and the rustle of tinfoil that meant Ryn was with a client in the middle of a color.

"You need to calm down; you need to focus." Ryn stood between Kiara and the door to the bedroom. Outwardly, Ryn was calm, but there was the slightest shift in her stance that told Kiara Ryn wasn't wholly certain Kiara could get herself back under control.

Oddly enough, that uncertainty pulled Kiara back into herself. Turning away, she sucked in several deep breaths. Her hands gripped the cool metal of the sink, the sensation grounded her, and she felt the itch in her gums slide away.

"Hey." Ryn touched Kiara's back. "I'm sorry. I didn't mean to make light of it. We'll figure it out, okay?"

Kiara turned, and Ryn held her arms out and wrapped up Kiara as tears started to fall. "Shhh, it's okay. It's just a class. You can retake it, or whatever." She kissed Kiara's temple.

Kiara clung tighter to Ryn. Her body shook, though now without danger of an uncontrolled shift.

☾

"Alpha-designate," Ryn mused. Kiara's head was in her lap, and Ryn was giving her a head massage that had Kiara absolutely lax with pleasure. "What does that even mean?"

"Mmmm, don't stop." Kiara closed her eyes. "It just means that, like, I'll be the next Alpha."

"Aren't you a little, I don't know, young to have your whole life planned out for you like that?"

Kiara shrugged—but carefully, because she didn't want to dislodge Ryn's clever fingers where they dug into her scalp. "It's always been that way. I'm the most powerful next to my dad, so it's my job to take over. I have to be the one to protect the pack, to keep us safe."

"But do you *have* to do it? Like, what happens if you don't want to? It's not like they can make you, right?"

"You can decline it. Alpha's more a title than a literal birthright. But no one does that. I mean, why would they?" Now Kiara twisted, reluctantly, out of Ryn's grip to face her.

"So you're gonna do it. No matter what happens in your life. No matter what other opportunities come up—things you wanna do, people?" Ryn added with a sardonic grin that didn't meet her dark eyes.

Kiara pressed her lips together; her thoughts spun in every direction at once. It had never occurred to her to think otherwise—why would it? But Ryn had obviously been thinking about it. And it sounded as if she saw a clear, dividing line between Kiara-as-Alpha and any kind of future the two of them could have together.

The thought of Ryn not being in her life—of losing Ryn to gain a title—clenched a hard fist around Kiara's heart. She couldn't imagine a future without Ryn. She couldn't imagine a future without a pack… could she?

Chapter Fourteen |

"Wow, so that's fucked up," Nathan commented after she'd returned downstairs and repeated the details of her phone call.

Ryn stood near one of Nathan's long windows with her arms wrapped around herself and her back to the rest of them. The urge to cross the room and wrap Ryn in her arms was strong enough that Kiara actually took two steps forward before she stopped herself, remembering that Ryn probably wouldn't appreciate the gesture.

"What do we do now?" Deanna asked. She and Jamie sat on the couch. Their hands were twined in Jamie's lap while Deanna stroked Arthur's head with her other hand. Jamie was looking at Ryn, who hadn't said a word since Kiara stopped speaking.

Cole rubbed his thumbs against his temples. "I don't know. Kiara made a good, strong case to the GNAAW rep." He gave Kiara an approving nod. "That doesn't mean GNAAW or the Huntsmen will respect it."

"I'm going to go." Ryn turned from the window and met each set of eyes in turn. "This is about me. We've heard that over and over again. It's my problem, not yours."

"Please don't."

They turned to look at Kiara; on each face was a different look of surprise. Kiara closed her eyes and swallowed against the tightness in her throat. "Please, please don't go."

"Kiara…"

"No, Ryn. I can't—" Kiara shook her head. "I can't let you go. I can't let you. They might kill you. They might have already, if we weren't there on Friday. Do you know how that feels?" Her voice was rising now; all the control she thought she had regained was gone. "That I might never have seen you again?"

"Kiara." The gentleness with which Ryn said her name broke something in Kiara.

"One more night. Give us one more night. You—you still haven't done Cole's hair. And it's a mess. There's a reason he hasn't had a date in a year." It was possibly the flimsiest excuse Kiara had ever come up with, but she couldn't let Ryn walk out that door if it meant that Kiara would never see her again and would never know what happened. "Stay, just for a bit longer, and we'll figure it out. Once we know it's done, once we know they won't come after you, then you can go."

"It's Sunday." Nathan spun idly on one of his barstools. "You might as well all stay for another night, right? Kiara can give GNAAW a few hours to get their shit figured out and then she can give her dad a call." He gave a wry grin. "I suspect Davis might want to go through him from now on. Presumably they'll have reached a solution or an agreement by Monday, and the rest of us," he said, gesturing to everyone but Ryn and Cole, "can get back to our regularly scheduled programming. One more night with the gang all together, what do you say?"

"I thought you were a pack, not a gang," Ryn pointed out. But she'd relaxed, was no longer looking as if she was prepared to bolt.

Relief left Kiara weak and she sank into the beanbag. Cole gave her shoulder a reassuring squeeze. Kiara grabbed his hand, holding on tight as she tried to get her emotions under control.

"Gang, pack, murder, parliament." Nathan waved his hands dismissively. Then, there was a sudden gleam in his eyes. "Besides, six is the perfect number of people to play the Game of Thrones board game."

On the couch, Deanna let out a groan. "Not that. Come on."

"Sorry," Nathan replied. "You promised on my birthday that you'd play it with me."

"I'm in, as long as we can order pizza for dinner," Cole said.

"You're not touching the Iron Throne with greasy pizza fingers," Nathan warned.

Jamie rolled her eyes. "We'll break for pizza. But we'd better grab a couple growlers of beer and maybe a bottle or two of wine. There's no way we're getting Deanna to play sober."

Deanna beamed at her girlfriend. "Love you, babe."

THREE HOURS LATER, KIARA REGRETTED everything. She wasn't sure how it had happened, but her reluctance to attack her friends had lost her Moat Cailin, and now she was trapped in the North. That's what she got for picking Stark. She knew better than to think the Starks had a chance to sit on the throne without suffering first. She could have built a fleet and gone around—she thought—but now it was too late. Nathan as the Greyjoys and Jamie as House Baratheon had filled the sea on either side of her with their own ships. Now she was just speculating from Winterfell. She was pretty sure her only choice was to make a deal with Nathan, but he was playing a despicable Greyjoy way too well for Kiara to consider it. He smirked every time he offered to let her through Moat Cailin, so he had something else up his sleeve.

She had no idea how he could torture her for this long and without looking remotely exhausted. If anything, he seemed energized as he refilled his beer glass.

"Can we stop now?" Jamie was lying flat on her back on the floor with her forearm thrown over her eyes. "Can we just… stop for a bit?"

"Oh, come on." Deanna poked her in the side. "You didn't mind half an hour ago when you took King's Landing from me."

"Well, I was winning then, wasn't I?" Jamie said sourly.

"It's actually not that bad," Cole remarked pushing his Dornish troops to Highgarden.

"I hate both of you."

"Cole's attacking you." Nathan jabbed Ryn with the cardboard Valyrian Steel Blade to get her attention. Ryn put her phone down and sighed, stared at the board, tried to find hope of holding onto her garrison.

"What's your address, Nathan? It's definitely pizza time." Cole stood and stretched. Kiara caught Nathan watching her brother and didn't miss the way he wet his lips as Cole's T-shirt stretched over his biceps.

Not quite focused, Nathan rattled off his address until Cole nodded and reached for his phone. Then, perhaps aware he had been staring, Nathan blushed and fled to the bathroom.

"Oh, thank god, it's break time." Jamie hauled herself up from the floor. "Though I think I'm going to need a refresher on the rules before we start up again."

"Do you have an extra hour?" Ryn muttered, still staring at the board. She reached forward as though to play a card and then thought better of it and pulled her hand back.

"Let's play some music," Deanna decided. "Staying still for too long is bad for you. So you know what that means…"

"No," Jamie whimpered. "Don't say it."

"Dance party!" Deanna crowed. She jumped to her feet and crossed the room to Nathan's impressive sound system.

Deanna fiddled with the buttons until Justin Bieber blasted through the apartment. Deanna let out a whoop and twirled to the beat. "Come on you guys! You can't resist the Bieb!"

"You only like him because he looks like a lesbian," Jamie argued, but she gamely rose to her feet and took a swig of her beer.

"I like you 'cause you look like a lesbian." Deanna gave a cheeky wink and grabbed Jamie's hands, forcing her to dance. "Come on, people, get dancing!"

"I mean, it is a catchy song," Ryn agreed. She unfolded herself from the floor beside the coffee table and bent, groaning at the stretch, to touch her toes. Kiara caught herself staring at Ryn's ass, which was encased in a borrowed pair of leggings. Heat rose in her cheeks when Ryn, as though she knew Kiara was staring, turned her head from where it was nearly pressed against her knees and winked.

Standing as abruptly as Nathan had, Kiara tore her gaze away and picked up her half-empty glass in a wild pretense of refilling it. "We need more beer," she announced to no one in particular and set the glass on the coffee table before fleeing into the kitchen, where there was another growler in the fridge.

Coming from the bathroom, Nathan met her there. His eyes were bright, and his face was flushed, and a few stray drops of water caught in his black hair told Kiara that he'd been splashing his face—probably with cold water. She might consider doing the same.

"I see Deanna's in charge of break time," Nathan observed. They turned to look at the living room, which had indeed turned into a dance party. Deanna bounced, her hands in the air, absolutely carefree. Jamie moved with a bit more self-consciousness beside her, but Kiara's cousin was grinning and, even as they watched, her movements loosened up. Cole was, absurdly, dancing with Arthur. He had the dog's front paws in his, and the two of them cavorted with surprising grace. Arthur's tail waved madly, and he barked as Ryn joined in.

Kiara turned away. She leaned against the island and faced the kitchen, avoiding the amused look Nathan sent her way.

"What happened with you two?" Nathan asked. His voice was low, barely a whisper, but this close, Kiara had no trouble picking it out despite the music.

Kiara shrugged, feigning disinterest with every ounce of her pride, though Nathan had seen her beg Ryn to stay. "The same thing that happens with everyone, eventually. We fit for a while. And then we didn't."

Nathan snorted. "Don't give me that bullshit. I think we're all past that."

"Fine." Kiara clenched her hands against the lip of the island. She gripped until she could feel the sharp edge dig into her palms. "What happened was, I nearly flunked out of university. What happened was, I barely spoke to my family for months. What happened was, I lost track of everything that was actually important to me—and worse, I was willing to give it up. All of it. All of this—" She jerked her head, indicating her brother and her cousin. "—for her. What happened was Ryn. And I can't let that happen again."

Nathan frowned. "That's probably a bit unfair, don't you think?"

Kiara stared at him, taken aback. He was supposed to be on her side. "No."

"I mean." Nathan shrugged. "It can't have been that one-sided, right?"

"Ryn had a lot less to lose. Trust me."

Nathan let what she'd said hang in the air between them. Kiara looked away as shame clawed up her throat. "I didn't mean it like that."

"How did you mean it?"

"I just…" Kiara glanced over her shoulder to where Ryn's arms were now twined around the neck of a furiously blushing Jamie while Cole and Deanna danced just feet away. "This is her life. Strangers and parties and, and, hair appointments. She doesn't have responsibilities, like me. She doesn't get it. She nearly had me running off with her. Giving up my pack, my position. That stuff doesn't matter to her."

"Family? Belonging?" Nathan shook his head. "I think those things matter to everyone."

"Not her," Kiara insisted. "Not to Ryn."

"She said that to you, did she?"

"No. But she didn't have to."

"Oh." Nathan nodded. "Kiara, the mind reader, sussed it out on her own."

"It's not like that! You're twisting what I'm saying."

"And you wouldn't know a thing about that, would you?"

"What does this even matter to you, Nathan? You don't know her."

He cocked his head. "I know you, though. You're the most bullheaded, stubborn, and selfish bisexual werewolf I've ever met."

"I'm not selfish." Kiara's face was hot, with anger now, not a blush. "You don't know half as much as you think you do."

"I'd say that makes two of us. Did anyone ever teach you how to have a real conversation, to actually listen to other people, or did this 'Alpha-designate' bullshit go to your head too early?"

They were nearly nose-to-nose now. Nathan's blue eyes bored into hers as Kiara tried to gain control of her temper so she didn't do something she'd regret.

Nathan opened his mouth, and Kiara was just *waiting* for it, when his phone buzzed on the kitchen island.

"Must be the pizza." He grabbed it, hitting the button to open the front door.

"Or not." Kiara was instantly on alert and sent Nathan a withering glare. "Did it occur to you that we're in hiding, and you just buzzed someone in without confirming who they are?"

Nathan began to retort, but paled as the implication of what Kiara said became clear to him. He swallowed. "I didn't think. I'm not used to this—"

Kiara brushed past him to the door. She waited in front of it, ears trained on the hallway outside. The elevator slid to a stop; the doors dinged open. Someone stepped through. The scent of pizza didn't follow.

Alarm spiked. Nathan came up behind her, and Kiara reached back, grabbed a handful of his T-shirt and yanked him forward. Outside the apartment, heels clipped along the hallway, came to a stop. The person knocked.

Kiara nodded at the peephole. "Do you know them?"

Nathan peered through; his shoulders were tight with tension. They relaxed as soon as he got a good look, only to tense again when the woman knocked for a second time.

"It's Amy. Fuck."

"Who is Amy?"

Nathan didn't answer, but attempted to wrestle Kiara out of the way. "Would you open the door?" he demanded.

Kiara narrowed her eyes and elbowed Nathan back. At the third knock she swung open the door a few inches and found herself staring at a tall woman with bright pink hair and precariously high heels. Her muscular legs were bare up to the short hem of her coat; her collar was flipped up. Kiara wondered if the coat hid lingerie or an axe tattoo.

"Who are you?" Kiara asked.

"Who are *you*?" the woman asked back.

"I'm supposed to be here. I don't think you are."

The woman laughed. "You're kind of a bitch; does anyone ever tell you that?"

"Every day." Kiara smiled. "Are we done here?" She couldn't smell anything unusual on the woman—no hint of weapons or the hair-raising scent of electricity that the cattle prods had carried—just the heady scent of expensive perfume and now impatience.

"Oh, *we're* done." The woman tried to shove past Kiara, obviously assuming that her size would be more than enough to move Kiara out of the way. When neither Kiara nor the door budged, the woman made a sharp noise. "What's going on? Seriously, who are you? And is—is Nathan having a party?" The woman's indignation seemed to mount as she peered over Kiara's head through the small opening of the door to the dance party beyond.

"Nathan!" The woman tried to push past Kiara again. "Nathan, what the fuck?"

Kiara finally allowed Nathan to wrestle past her. "Amy, I'm sorry."

"Did you forget about our date?"

"There's been a lot going on. I didn't realize… It completely slipped my mind."

On the counter, Nathan's phone buzzed again. Kiara left Nathan to deal with Amy, fairly certain that she wasn't a threat—at least not to anyone other than Nathan—and answered. "Who're you?" she demanded.

"Uhhh… Mitilini's Pizza?" a male voice answered hesitantly. Kiara buzzed him in, then watched Nathan shoo Amy out the door.

"I don't see how it's not a good time. You're obviously having a party. So… what? I'm good enough to fuck but not to meet your friends? Is that it?" Her voice rose as she fought to be heard over Adam Lambert.

"No, Amy, it's not that, really. I wish I could explain, but—" Nathan shook his head. "Let's reschedule, okay? I'm so sorry, I forgot that our date was tonight. It wasn't on purpose. I promise."

"It's a family thing," Kiara informed the woman.

"Yeah, I can see the resemblance." The woman stepped back from the door. "You're both assholes."

"Amy, I'm sorry!" Nathan called after her. She gave him the finger as she waited for the elevator. The doors popped open, and the guy from Mitilini's stepped out.

"Pizza's here!" Kiara yelled over her shoulder. The look Amy sent her before she stepped in the elevator was so venomous Kiara wondered if Nathan had a bezoar on hand.

Chapter Fifteen |

"WAS THAT AMY I HEARD?" Deanna asked as they crowded around the island, where everyone fought for a slice of their favorite pizza.

"Yeah." Nathan hadn't joined in the fray. "We were supposed to have a date tonight. And I forgot about it."

"I'm sorry." Ryn gave his shoulder a sympathetic squeeze as she reached for a napkin. "She'll come around though, hot guy like you."

Nathan barked out a laugh. "Yeah, maybe if someone hadn't been a total *dick* to her." He looked pointedly at Kiara.

Kiara sniffed and grabbed for a slice of meat lover's before it all disappeared. "Sorry I'm careful. It's only that I don't know if you noticed, we're being *hunted*."

"Whatever." Nathan sighed and took a slice of the pineapple pizza. "It wasn't that serious or anything."

Deanna laughed. "Are they ever?"

Nathan glared at her. "It's a little hard to have a serious relationship when all this werewolf bullshit keeps invading. Literally."

Jamie winced. "I'm sorry."

Deanna nodded, looking sheepish. "Me too."

"It's fine." Nathan dropped his plate on the counter, barely having taken a bite. "It's fine." He picked up Arthur's leash. "I'm going for a walk. I'll be back."

As the front door closed, the bite of pepperoni and bacon smothered in cheese in Kiara's mouth suddenly tasted like sawdust.

Across the island, Ryn was watching Kiara with a too-knowing expression.

"Have you heard anything from Dad?" Kiara asked Cole, abruptly changing the subject. He shook his head. She wasn't surprised—he'd have said something if he had. "I'll give him a call." She snagged another piece of the meat lover's and her phone and went upstairs.

"We can't keep playing without Nathan… so come on, handsome, let me give you that haircut." Kiara heard Ryn's suggestion to Cole before she tuned them out.

"Dad." He answered on the third ring. "Has GNAAW talked to you?"

"Yes." Her father's voice sounded weary. "Kiara, you realize your actions affect the rest of us, right? This isn't happening in a bubble."

"He was an idiot, Dad. He didn't even know what had happened in the alley. He—"

"He's someone we have to respect and not someone we say no to."

"Dad!" Kiara responded, horrified. "He wanted us to turn Ryn over to the Huntsmen! For no reason. She hasn't *done* anything."

"You cannot keep protecting this person," her father said. She could almost see his clenched teeth. "She is not pack. She is not anyone's pack. You cannot risk all of us for one lone wolf. I will not allow it."

"What about last year?" Kiara shot back. "Cole and I risked ourselves for Deanna. She wasn't pack."

"Did you forget about Jamie?"

"No, I just—" Kiara rubbed at the frown lines growing on her forehead. "Taryn is innocent—completely, utterly innocent. We don't know anything about the Huntsmen. We didn't even know if they were real until three days ago. And now we're just supposed to give up one of ours to them without a fuss?"

"Not one of ours."

"She's a wolf, Dad. She belongs with us before she belongs with them. Do you even know what they're going to do with her?"

"Do you?"

"I know enough."

"Unfortunately, Kiara, you are not the Alpha of this pack. I am. And you *will* do as I say. Tomorrow, Mr. Davis will contact you again, and when he does I expect you to do exactly as he says. Am I clear?"

Kiara pressed her lips together. "Yes."

"I'm sorry about this." Her father gentled his voice. "I know you're not happy about it and I know it's not fair. But we are in an incredibly tricky position, and I have to look out for the well-being of my pack before that of a stranger. You'll understand one day."

"I'll call you tomorrow, after it's done."

"Thank you, Kiara. Say hi to your brother for me."

"Say hi to Mom." Kiara hung up the phone. She stared at it: the pink case, the fingerprint-covered screen. She picked up the small garbage can Nathan kept beside his bed. She held the phone over the garbage can and carefully, deliberately, crushed it in her right hand so that all the pieces fell neatly into the garbage. Then, she slid the can back into place.

Chapter Sixteen |

"GNAAW WANTS US TO STAY put for now." Kiara answered Jamie's unspoken question as she came down the stairs.

Nathan had returned and twisted to look up at her from where he was tidying. "Like, stay here?"

Kiara nodded. "Not all of us. But Ryn should. And I've got plenty of sick days."

"Here," Nathan repeated, "like, my house specifically?"

Kiara blanked. "Yes." When she'd destroyed her phone upstairs she hadn't had a specific plan—she still didn't. All she knew was that she wasn't going to let Ryn out of her sight and she definitely wasn't going to let the Huntsmen take her. For now, staying at Nathan's seemed like the safest bet. No one else knew where they were, and all she'd told her father in their initial phone call was that they were with a friend of Deanna's. Deanna had a lot of friends. It could be anyone. They could be anywhere in the city.

Ryn didn't look up as she swept Cole's hair off the cement floor of the apartment, though the line of her back was tense.

"They're meeting with the Huntsmen tomorrow. They'll talk about this mess then. GNAAW will put it right, and then they'll let us know when we can go." Kiara was improvising. She had no idea what would happen when Davis was unable to contact her. She was being stupid, incredibly, recklessly stupid, but she couldn't bring herself to tell them the truth: that her father wanted them to give Ryn up, and that GNAAW wouldn't lift a finger to keep Ryn safe from the Huntsmen.

The whole thing was making Kiara sick. She'd been told all her life that GNAAW was there to protect wolves, that she could rely on the system, that she could trust it to keep her safe. Finding out that simply wasn't true was turning her world upside down, and she was starting to understand Ryn's instant distrust for any self-proclaimed benevolent authority.

"Great." Deanna was cheerful as she helped Nathan clear away the pizza.

"Yeah, great," Ryn echoed.

Kiara nodded, not meeting anyone's eye as she crossed to the washroom. She locked the door behind her, turned on the taps, and stared at her reflection. Her makeup had long since washed off. Without her styling products, her hair was a puffy mess. It wasn't curly, like Deanna's, so the humidity added volume without control. She could have asked Ryn, of course. Judging from how the rest of the occupants of the loft looked relatively put together, Ryn wasn't opposed to sharing—or charging.

The instant she had the thought, Kiara dropped her head in shame, unable to meet her own eyes. Ryn's job was as entirely legitimate as Kiara's work as a mechanical engineer. Ryn was right to charge for her services, and Deanna had saved the day when she'd been able to mitigate Ryn's loss of income.

"Hurry up, K," Jamie called from the other room. "It's your turn!"

☾

JAMIE, DEANNA, AND RYN HAD gone upstairs to bed twenty minutes ago. They were asleep now; Jamie and Deanna's breaths came smooth and even, in sync with one another, while the rustle of Ryn's sleeping bag betrayed her uneasy rest.

On the couch, Kiara pulled her blanket to her chin and willed herself to sleep. She'd need a clear head tomorrow, and who knew when she'd next feel safe enough to sleep.

In the hallway, the elevator opened. Kiara held her breath until the sound of Arthur's claws on the floor, accompanied by two pairs of feet, reassured her that Nathan and Cole had returned from taking Arthur out for a last-of-the-day walk.

They let themselves into the apartment. Arthur trotted straight up the stairs and settled with a happy groan next to Jamie and Deanna on the air mattress, which wheezed at the added weight.

"I think about getting a dog." Cole hung up his coat and followed Nathan into the kitchen, which was lit by the dim stove light. "But it isn't really fair—Kiara works long days, and since I work shifts…" He shrugged regretfully. "Can't keep a dog cooped up all day. Arthur is lucky he has Deanna."

"Deanna's lucky she has Arthur," Nathan joked. "Well, we are all lucky to have Arthur."

Cole hummed.

There was a long silence. Kiara let out a slow breath and closed her eyes. Cole would know she was awake, but they were used to politely ignoring the parts of each other's lives that they couldn't help but overhear. Werewolf manners—if you weren't supposed to hear or smell, you pretended you hadn't. It had made their teenage years much more bearable.

"I'm sorry about earlier. With your date."

Nathan gave a rueful laugh. "What can you do, right? This stuff kind of comes first these days."

"I wish it didn't. You shouldn't have to put your life on hold for our politics, our problems."

"It's not all bad. There are perks."

"Slumber parties?"

"Slumber parties with enough people to play Game of Thrones," Nathan corrected.

"Right." Cole's voice was warm.

Another silence followed.

"It wasn't serious."

"Hmm?"

"Amy. She wasn't—we weren't. Serious. I don't really do serious. Or, I haven't."

"No?" An uptick of interest now, discernible only to Kiara by the cautious catch in Cole's breath.

"No. It's not that... it's not that I wouldn't. But, you know, other stuff comes first. Deanna. Work. Family—I mean, that's Deanna again. And Arthur. And Jamie."

"Family is important. I get that."

"I know. I know you do. Obviously there's the whole werewolf-pack-thing, which, from my understanding, is like regular family times a million, with more shedding."

Cole snorted.

"Most people don't get it. They wanna be, like, The One." Nathan paused. "It hurts people when they can't be that for me."

"Is that a warning?"

"It's..." Nathan licked his lips. "It's just a fact. You should—I want you to have the facts."

"You can take the librarian out of the library."

"Hah. Yeah. Something like that."

"Why don't we try something like this..."

A sharp intake of breath. Two hearts pounded. A moan, muffled against lips.

Kiara buried her face in her pillow and smiled.

"ARE YOU SURE YOU DON'T need us to stay?" Cole lingered in Nathan's front doorway. "I can switch my shift, if you want."

"It's fine." Kiara plastered a smile on her face. "You're probably sick of this place anyway." Deanna, Arthur, and Jamie had already left, and now all she had to do was get Cole and then Nathan, out the door.

"I don't know…" Cole's head turned to the bathroom, where Nathan was showering. "It's growing on me."

Kiara snorted a laugh. "Yes, it's clearly the *apartment* that's growing on you."

Cole shrugged casually, not denying the implication. "GNAAW will call you, then?" His eyes, the same honey gold as hers, searched her face. "And they'll have sorted it out so Ryn won't have to worry about the Huntsmen coming after her?"

"Yep." Kiara nodded. "That's what Dad said." She didn't like lying to Cole. She never had, not really. There just hadn't been reason to, since whatever mess she found herself in, he was at her side or not too far behind her. But she wanted him and Jamie to have completely plausible deniability. Kiara wasn't going to let any harm come to her pack, but she wasn't going to let any come to Ryn, either.

"Okay." Cole nodded slowly. "I left some cash upstairs on the dresser."

Nathan emerged from the bathroom in a billow of steam. "I'm flattered, but you know we just slept together, not *slept* together." He wriggled past them, clad only in a blue towel that hung low on his hips.

Cole watched him until he walked up the stairs, before his focus returned to Kiara. "On the dresser," he repeated. "In case you need it."

"Thanks. I'm sure we won't, but I appreciate it," Kiara said mildly.

"All right. Call if you need us."

"Will do." Kiara pointedly held open the door. "I'll let you know how it goes."

Cole dropped a kiss on her forehead before he stepped through the door. "Tell Ryn thanks for the haircut."

"Uh-huh." As he finally went down the hall, Kiara closed the door. Cole knew something was up, obviously. But she appreciated that he was letting her take care of it.

"Holy shit." Nathan's voice echoed from the loft. "This is like, a lot of cash. What does he think you're going to need it for? Bankrolling a movie?"

"Don't you have to go to work?" Kiara asked.

"I'm going, I'm going!" Nathan, hair still damp, barreled down the stairs.

"What did I tell you about mousse?" Ryn asked in exasperation as he ducked into the kitchen to grab a banana.

"I'll use it tomorrow. Promise." Nathan flashed Ryn a grin, blew Kiara a kiss, and was out the door.

Kiara locked the door behind Nathan and returned to the kitchen, where she'd left her coffee. Ryn sat on one of the bar stools across the island and didn't look up from her phone.

Kiara lifted her mug up to take a sip, but the thought of coffee suddenly made her ill. She set it down, and her eyes focused on the clock on the microwave. Seven thirty-six. She tapped her nails against the side of the mug. Ryn glared at her.

Kiara stopped tapping. She looked at the clock again. Seven thirty-nine.

She picked up her mug and dumped the coffee in the sink, rinsed it, and set it on the counter.

Seven forty-one.

Fuck it.

"Okay." She blew out a nervous breath. Ryn looked up from her phone. "Get your stuff. Let's go."

"I thought we were waiting for—"

"I lied. We can't stay here. Davis is supposed to call me and arrange a meeting so I can hand you over. But I won't. So we need to go."

Ryn stared at her. Kiara was already moving out of the kitchen. "Get your stuff."

"And where are we going to go?"

"I don't know."

There was silence, and from halfway up the stairs she turned and looked at Ryn. Ryn was studying her; the look on her face was so intense that Kiara felt pinned in place against the wall.

"All right," Ryn said, finally. She rose from the barstool and gathered her things.

Kiara pulled open Nathan's closet and rummaged until she found a backpack. She tossed her purse inside, grabbed the cash from the dresser—she didn't bother to count it; the rainbow of colors assured her that it was more than enough—and stole a couple of Nathan's shirts while she was at it. She left behind her outfit from Friday, figuring she'd have no need of a clubbing dress.

Down the stairs again, she picked up the set of Nathan's house keys that Deanna had left for them, and in their place in the little dish at the front door she dropped a note for Nathan and the others. It didn't say much, simply "Sorry." She figured they'd understand.

"Ready." Ryn appeared with her duffel bag slung over her shoulder. "You good?"

Kiara took one last look around the apartment. "Yeah." She had everything she needed. The cash from Cole meant that she wouldn't need to use her debit or credit cards—and as the bank would have been her first stop, otherwise, that knocked something off her list. "Let's get out of here."

Ryn grabbed her bike and followed Kiara out the door.

Chapter Seventeen |

Ten years ago...

"I've got a friend who lives in Spain." Ryn added fruit to the shopping cart for the sangria they planned to make for the party Ryn was hosting that night. "He says it's amazing. They've got hostels like, everywhere, and the beaches are gorgeous."

"I can't imagine you in a swimming suit," Kiara said honestly, smiling at the mental image of Ryn in a bikini—somehow it just didn't look right.

"Love, I don't wear bathing suits." Ryn wiggled her eyebrows. "The only way to swim is naked."

"What if there were other people!" Kiara tried to act scandalized, but all she could think of was what Ryn would look like emerging from the waves with salt water running in rivulets down her sides.

"Pay attention." Ryn thwacked Kiara lightly with the package of Solo cups she picked up. "I can *smell* your mind wandering."

"Oh yeah?" Kiara glanced around to make sure that no one was watching, and backed Ryn into a display. "Care to do something about it?" she asked flirtatiously.

Ryn's eyes gleamed wickedly and she palmed Kiara's breast through her shirt. Kiara's nipple hardened instantly at the contact and she bit back a moan when Ryn ran her thumb over the tip. "What I'm saying is, we could go to Spain."

Kiara made a soft noise of agreement and her breath hitched. "The semester's almost over."

"Why wait, though?" Ryn leaned forward and brushed her lips over the delicate shell of Kiara's ear. "Why not go now?"

"Well, the party." Kiara was finding it hard to think.

"All right, after the party. We can give it a week—I've got clients I shouldn't cancel on." Ryn sucked the lobe of Kiara's ear into her mouth. "But then, let's go, me and you. Leave this behind. Run wild with me, Kiara."

Kiara shivered, her entire body pulsing with need—for Ryn, for the freedom Ryn promised. "Okay," she agreed. "Okay."

☾

IT WAS THE FIRST WARM night in months. They'd spent the evening looking at flights, trying to figure out where the closest hostel to the airport was. Kiara had bought them both backpacks the day before and surprised Ryn with them when she'd come home from work. They'd decided to celebrate by going for a run as soon as the sun had set. Usually they drove out of the city to shift and run, but Kiara had sold her car to Sophia three days earlier, and Ryn had convinced her that one night running in the city wouldn't do any harm. Since she'd been right the last time, Kiara had caved.

Do you think there are Spanish werewolves? Kiara loped easily behind Ryn, letting her lead the way as they wove down the side streets.

Well, there are part-Korean ones, so I'd assume so. Ryn lolled out her tongue in a wolfish grin.

Good point.

They were nearing the end of their run, heading toward Ryn's apartment. Kiara thought she should probably swing by her dorm room before they left for Spain—anything really important she'd long since started keeping at Ryn's, but there might have been something they'd overlooked.

Ryn increased their pace, her tail shot straight out behind her like the tail of a comet, and Kiara let the joy of a run wash over her. Running with her family had never felt like this. Something about being with Ryn made Kiara's blood sing, made her want to howl and leap and hunt. Weeks ago they'd brought down a moose, and it had been the most exciting night of Kiara's life.

Careful, Kiara warned as they grew closer to the university. It was a bit more dangerous to run as a wolf here; students who were out late drinking or studying didn't have the same regard for normal hours as the rest of the city's population. Kiara usually liked to shift back well before they got this close, but they'd shifted from home tonight so they had nothing to wear, and Kiara wasn't going to wander through her own neighborhood naked.

Quit worrying. Ryn's ears flicked irritably, and she put on an extra burst of speed to distance herself from Kiara.

Kiara's lips curled back from her teeth in a silent snarl, since they were too exposed for her to draw any attention by making a real one. Ryn disappeared around a corner, and Kiara had no choice but to follow.

She thought she'd lost Ryn, and Kiara had a second of panic that mounted when she heard voices ahead.

"Dude, that guy was a total faggot. Did you see the way he was looking at me?" A young man in a backward baseball cap and hockey jersey shuddered. "Like, whatever, be gay, but don't be gay in my changing room."

"That's disgusting," his companion agreed. "You should talk to the gym owner. Gay guys need their own gym. There's no way I'm joining now."

"You're just gonna make me go alone? What if the fag jumps me in the shower, huh?"

"Better not drop the soap!"

A low growl echoed from the shadows of a garage. Kiara froze; fear turned her bones to ice.

The growl grew louder, and the men slowed. "Did you hear that?"

Ryn emerged from the shadows behind them. Her ears were flat to her skull, and her fangs were bared. The first man turned around and let out a high-pitched yelp when he saw what was advancing on him. His companion turned and then tripped over his own feet in his hurry to escape.

"What the fuck, what the fuck!"

Ryn!

Ryn ignored Kiara and stalked closer to the men. The one who'd fallen grabbed at his friend, frantic for a hand up, but the man was walking backward with his hands held out in front of him saying, "Good doggy, good dog…"

"Mike, that's not a fucking dog!" The one on the ground finally scrambled to his feet and ran. His friend continued to try to back away, too scared to turn his back on Ryn.

Ryn opened her mouth, let the man see the saliva dripping from her jaws. He choked on a scream and, when Ryn lunged forward, he turned tail and ran as fast as his legs could carry him.

Oh, come on, Ryn rolled her eyes at Kiara when she turned back. *It was just a bit of fun. Those homophobic assholes deserved to be scared.*

"WHAT THE FUCK, RYN! You can't do that!"

"Get off my back, Kiara, it wasn't that big a deal."

"'Not that big a deal'? Ryn, they saw you. You let them. You *wanted them to*!"

"Calm down. No one got hurt. They were drunk, anyway—you could smell cheap rum from a mile away."

"No, Ryn. This is bad. I can't believe you did that."

"Jesus." Ryn threw up her hands in exasperation. "It was fine. Stop freaking out."

"This is serious!" Kiara slammed her hands on the kitchen table. "You need to take this seriously!"

"*You* need to lighten up."

"Do you understand what you just did? We have *rules*. And you broke the biggest one! On purpose! How do you not see what the problem is?"

"There's no problem." Ryn dropped onto the living room couch and picked up the book she was reading from the coffee table. "We're gonna be gone in like a week. I don't get what the big deal is."

"Of course you don't. Nothing's a big deal to you. You think you can just do whatever you want and not have any consequences."

"Get off your high horse, Kiara. It's getting old."

"Fuck you." Kiara twisted her hands in her hair; panic felt thick in her throat. God, what if GNAAW found out? What would they do? What would happen to her pack, to her dad?

"You know, no one's asking you to stick around." Ryn snapped her book closed. "Run back to your pack and your title and stop telling me how to live my life."

"Yeah, cause it's such a great life." Sarcasm coated Kiara's words. "You've got a real good thing going here on your own."

"At least when I'm on my own, no one's nagging at me."

"You're such a bitch."

"You're done slumming it then, I guess?"

Angry tears stung the corners of Kiara's eyes. "Stop acting like you're the wounded party here. You *exposed* us."

"I didn't expose 'us'; I exposed *me*. In case you forgot, I'm not a part of your Assembly. I don't owe anyone anything, I didn't agree to spend my life lurking in the shadows, I didn't ask for *this*." Ryn gestured to her body. "This happened to me. I didn't choose it. And I wouldn't change it—but some accident of birth doesn't mean that I owe a bunch of old dudes I've never met my loyalty or my obedience. I decide what I do with my body. Not them."

Under the anger, Kiara's heart ached for Ryn and how she'd grown up bereft of werewolf culture. "Ryn, this isn't just about you. You put all of us at risk!"

"I won't live my life afraid, Kiara."

"It's not fear; it's caution. It's not taking stupid risks just for the hell of it."

Ryn laughed. "What risk? They were drunk and stupid, and no one is going to believe them. Werewolves aren't real, Kiara."

"Except we *are*, and you don't seem to understand that your actions affect the rest of us!"

"I understand all right, I just don't care."

"You never care. I get that now. I just wish I'd seen that sooner." Kiara stormed out of the kitchen and into the bedroom. She grabbed one of the new backpacks she'd bought, and stuffed her belongings into it.

"So that's it? You're going to leave?"

"I don't see any reason to stay."

Ryn stood in the doorway, still holding her book, and inarticulate with rage. "If you walk out that door, don't you dare come back."

"Trust me," Kiara lifted the bag over her shoulder. "I won't." She shoved past Ryn, knocking her into the wall. Ryn snarled and flung the book—something heavy and hardcover—at Kiara's retreating head. It missed and left a dent in the wall to Kiara's left.

Kiara didn't wait to see what Ryn was going to throw next, just slammed the door on her way out.

Chapter Eighteen |

THE HALLWAY WAS EERILY QUIET. At this time of day, Kiara'd expected at least a few people headed off to work. They rode the elevator in silence down to the garage level. She was taking Nathan's car, something she knew he wouldn't thank her for, but the car keys had been on the same keychain as the house keys, and it had seemed too perfect to resist. Besides, once they got far enough away she'd dump it and find something else.

For the first time since that night at Kings of Hearts, there was no tension between her and Ryn. The silence as the elevator moved could have been awkward, but their shared purpose burned away any discomfort. Kiara felt herself falling back in sync with Ryn. A part of her worried at the ease of it. Would it be as easy to pull back if—when—she had to? But she'd cross that bridge when she came to it. For now, she had one goal, and that was to get Ryn as far from the Huntsmen and GNAAW as she could.

The elevator doors opened, and they stepped out into the empty lobby. The parkade was through another door, where the pop of lime-green glowed bright in the concrete lobby, and Kiara pushed through it. She jogged down the few stairs before she stepped out into the parkade. "Nathan has a Mazda3 hatchback," Kiara said. "I don't know where he parks it, but—"

"Kiara." Ryn's voice was sharp. Kiara froze, all her senses suddenly on alert. They weren't alone.

Kiara turned toward the door as Ryn walked back up the stairs. The door opened before either of them could reach it, and the Huntress from the club stepped through. She held the same weapon as last time, and a chill went up Kiara's spine as she imagined what effect the cattle prod might have.

Ryn growled, low and fierce, and Kiara's gums itched with the promise of fangs, but they backed up as the woman moved forward.

A noise above her jerked Kiara's attention upward. A metal catwalk, painted purple, ran across the top of the parkade, and a man stood in the middle with a rifle trained on the two of them.

"Hey, packwolf." The woman's voice drew Kiara's attention back to her. "You can go."

Kiara didn't bother to respond. She and Ryn had moved until they stood side by side. Her ears caught three more Huntsmen inching toward them from the parked cars; the too-careful placement of their feet on the concrete betrayed them as something other than civilian. Kiara touched Ryn's hand, indicating for her to stay still, as Kiara stepped so that she and Ryn now stood back to back, and Kiara could look the approaching Huntsmen in the eye.

Dressed in black like some sort of militia, two had guns and the third a prod to match the woman's. Kiara recognized one, the man whose nose Ryn had bloodied. He kept his gun and his gaze steady on her as he met her eyes. His nose was still bandaged—probably broken, Kiara thought with no small sense of satisfaction. His lips curled up in a smirk, and when she still didn't look away he blew her a kiss. She bared her teeth and imagined breaking his nose again.

There was a large white van parked haphazardly in the middle of the parkade. The only windows seemed to be in the front, and the back doors gaped open. It was obvious that whatever they were planning to do with Ryn involved taking her to another location. Had they had the van with them outside the club? If she and Jamie hadn't happened to have been there, would Ryn have been taken completely unaware and stuffed in the back?

No, not likely, Kiara thought as Ryn's growling grew louder. Ryn wouldn't let anyone take her somewhere she didn't want to go.

"I don't want to hurt any of you," Ryn warned. The men approaching slowed and now ringed them in a loose circle.

"Yeah? Is that what you told Matt when you threw him into a wall?" one of them taunted. He spat, and the glob of mucus and saliva slid down the toe of Ryn's polished oxford. "You fuckin' lycans fractured his ribs."

"It was *this* 'fucking lycan' who threw Matt into a wall," Kiara corrected him, gesturing at herself without taking her eyes off the three men. The word 'lycan' left a sour taste in her mouth. She *was* a werewolf; she didn't *have* lycanthropy. There was no disease, nothing that needed a cure or a diagnosis.

"Not what I heard," the man replied. "I heard it was the lone one. They're dangerous, and this just proves it."

Kiara's gaze retuned to the man with the broken nose, who was now standing directly in front of her. Ryn hadn't been able to throw Matt into a wall because she'd been busy keeping Broken Nose Guy on his knees—why did everyone seem to think otherwise? She wasn't sure what she expected him to do, correct his buddy or indicate somehow that he knew otherwise, but all he did was wink

Kiara's temper was gradually overcoming her initial fear. Whatever was going on, whatever frame-job bullshit was culminating in this showdown, she was tired of it. She'd had enough uncertainty stuck in Nathan's apartment for three days. She wasn't going to wait and see what was going to happen.

"We just want the lone wolf." As the woman came down the steps, her boots echoed in the cavernous space. "Help us take her, and no one will get hurt."

Help them? At Kiara's back, Ryn tensed. Kiara laughed. She dropped the backpack, silently mourned the loss of her T-shirt, and shifted.

It didn't take more than a split second—Kiara hadn't made any idle threats to Davis. Second to her father, she had the most power in her pack, and that meant human-to-wolf in the blink of an eye. Fur exploded across her body, and then she was on all fours with the torn remains of her clothing falling from her.

"Careful!" the woman shouted as suddenly every gun in the place was trained on Kiara. "Don't hurt that one. Use the tranq gun or the prods, but *do not* shoot her."

Kiara bared her teeth, lips curled in a vicious snarl. She feinted toward the man closest to her, the one who'd spit, and he stumbled back with a yelp. The other two clutched their weapons tighter.

In this form, all her senses were dialed up to twelve. She was aware of the currents of recycled air being pumped through the ventilation system ruffling the fur along her sides. She sensed the change when one of the men to her side moved closer. His heartbeat pounded; the scent of his fear tasted hot and metallic in the back of her throat. He was just a distraction. Her ears flicked back, hearing the gentle scuff as one of the men on the catwalk adjusted his footing, hearing his breath sigh out as he lined up his gun—tranq.

Kiara leapt in a blur of motion. She drove her shoulder into the man who was inching closer. He crashed to the ground; the breath was driven out of him, and his prod clattered from his fingers. The sharp sent of urine ballooned in the air as she snapped her jaws shut a hairsbreadth from his naked throat.

She dove off of him. The tranq dart passed harmlessly through the fur on her tail as she turned on a dime and went straight for the other two men.

Ryn used the distraction, ran, and ducked between two parked cars.

As soon as Kiara moved toward him, the spitter turned tail and fled, running straight out the parkade's emergency exit. Broken Nose held his ground and fired a warning shot. The bullet was real. It plowed into the concrete inches away from Kiara's front paws. The scent of silver made her nose wrinkle and her ears flatten against her skull. Her throat vibrated in a steady growl.

Kiara had to keep the focus away from Ryn and she had to do it, she hoped, without getting shot. Broken Nose smelled of sweat, adrenaline, and nerves all twined around an eager sort of glee as he trained the barrel of his gun on her. His eyes gleamed. Despite what the Huntress had ordered, he wanted to shoot.

From above her came the same soft sigh from the marksman as he lined up his shot, then a puff as the dart exited the gun. Kiara dove left. Her claws skidded against the concrete as she swung around. She recognized her mistake immediately. Broken Nose was now between her and Ryn and, with a smirk in Kiara's direction, he leveled his gun right at Ryn, where she crouched between cars.

Kiara didn't let Broken Nose revel in his smugness. The man seemed to have forgotten who—*what*—he was dealing with. The second he glanced toward Ryn, Kiara attacked. She went for his legs; her powerful jaws closed over his calf and sank in until muscle filled her mouth. He shrieked. The barrel of the gun cracked against Kiara's muzzle as he tried to bat her away. Pain sparked along her face, but she held on and began to drag him backward. He slammed the gun into her face again before she yanked his feet out from under him and he crashed to the floor. The gun went spinning.

"Shoot her, shoot her!" he screamed, spittle flying from his mouth.

Kiara hadn't forgotten about the man on the catwalk. In the split second he took to pull the trigger, she leapt out of the way, and instead of sinking into her flank the tranq struck Broken Nose in his injured leg. The drug hit his system, and he went limp.

The taste of his blood was hot and sweet in her throat.

She barreled up the stairs to the catwalk as the shooter began to reload. She reached him before he had a chance and shoved him off the balcony to land with a crash on the cement below.

Ryn had scooped up Broken Nose's gun and stepped over him. She faced the Huntress with the gun held down at her side.

"We're going to leave," she told her calmly. "And you're not going to follow us."

Kiara leapt down from the catwalk and padded to Ryn's side.

"This is a mistake." The Huntress spoke directly to Kiara, as though Ryn was the one who couldn't respond. "She's dangerous. She'll hurt someone, eventually, someone innocent. The lone ones have no control."

Kiara flashed her fangs. The only people who were going to get hurt were the ones who were trying to hurt them, and she didn't see any innocence in that.

"We're going to leave," Ryn repeated. She bent down, keeping her eyes and the gun on the Huntress as she grabbed their two bags. She slung the bigger one over her shoulder and stuffed Kiara's backpack into the basket of her bike as she picked it up off the ground.

One hand on the handlebars, and the other still holding the gun steady, she backed away from the woman. Kiara stood her ground, hackles high, until Ryn opened the door of the parkade. With one last withering snarl, Kiara turned and loped out to Ryn.

Chapter Nineteen |

THE SECOND KIARA JOINED HER, Ryn threw a leg over her bike and started to pedal. Kiara raced easily alongside, grateful that the winter month meant that it was still relatively dark. As a wolf, she was just as tall as Ryn's bike and several times wider. There wasn't any mistaking her for a dog, but there was no time for her to shift back. They needed to get away, far away, as fast as they could.

Ryn sped through the streets, not speaking. Kiara wasn't familiar enough with Vancouver to know where they were headed, but she trusted Ryn. Despite the violence they'd just fled, Kiara reveled in the joy of running free through the city. The air was chill and damp, and the pavement was cold and wet under her paws. She could hear the lazy rumble of traffic as the city awoke: folks trudging toward buses or unchaining bikes. Ryn turned sharply into a back alley as they entered a more populated neighborhood, and Kiara kept to the shadows. She and Jamie and Cole would go into the woods when they felt the urge to shift, the need to run flat-out and on all fours. The last time Kiara had been reckless enough to run as she was now, with the sun edging toward the horizon and regular people pressing in on all sides, had been with Ryn.

Ryn finally pulled her bike to a stop in the overhang leading to an underground parkade. Kiara's ears pricked forward, listening for anyone who might be close enough to stumble across them. Not hearing anyone, she padded to Ryn's side and gave one quick shake of her coat to clear away the dampness of the early morning before shifting back.

The instant her pelt vanished, Kiara shivered. The wet pavement was now freezing cold against her bare feet, and she wrapped her arms around herself.

"Here." Ryn tossed Kiara her backpack, and Kiara pulled out the spare change of clothes she'd packed. She pulled on a pair of stretch leggings and a long-sleeved shirt.

Her shoes were still in Nathan's parkade, and Kiara made a mental note to include flip-flops in her bug-out-bags in future. Now that they were far enough away from the Huntsmen, Kiara's adrenaline rush faded. Shifting back and forth always took energy, and that combined with the fight and flight—and Kiara's restless night—meant exhaustion was rapidly settling in.

"What now?" The question slipped out before Kiara realized she intended to ask it. She wanted to take it back, not wanting Ryn to see how at a loss she was. She wanted Ryn to pull her in and hold her close. She wanted to go back to when everything was normal. *Would you really, though? Wouldn't you do it all over again if you knew you'd get Ryn?* Kiara didn't have an answer.

Ryn swung her leg over the center bar of her bike and patted the seat behind her. "Hop on. We'll find a hotel."

Kiara only hesitated for a moment before she complied. Ryn kicked off, and Kiara held herself steady as the bike lurched forward.

THE HOTEL LOBBY WAS GRIMY, and Kiara tried not to think about her bare feet against the cracked linoleum. However, the lack of care meant that no one questioned why she was without shoes or looked twice at the fact that she paid in cash.

Kiara took the keys the disinterested clerk handed her and joined Ryn at the elevator bank. For once, Ryn's face was drawn. The elevator doors opened, and they stepped in. Kiara hit the button for the sixth floor, and they rode in silence.

The room wasn't much better than the lobby, but at least the floor was covered with a thin, worn carpet. It was probably just as—if not more—filthy as the linoleum, but at least it wasn't cold.

Though it had been at least an hour earlier and shouldn't have carried over with the shift, Kiara could still taste blood in her mouth. The second Ryn locked the door, Kiara ducked into the bathroom.

She hadn't thought to grab a toothbrush from Nathan's, let alone toothpaste, and decided she'd have to visit the convenience store in the lobby before the day was out. For now, she rinsed her mouth with tap water.

When she came out of the room, Ryn had propped her bike against the door. It wasn't the most effective barricade, but it would slow someone down.

Kiara dropped her backpack beside the room's queen-sized bed. Ryn pulled the curtains across the window and sank into a chair. Kiara ran a hand over her face and settled onto the bed.

"Now what?" Ryn asked. Her tired eyes met Kiara's.

"I don't know," Kiara admitted. "I don't know how they knew where we were."

Neither of them spoke after that. Kiara wasn't sure there was anything more to be said. Her entire body ached; she wanted nothing more than to curl up on the mattress and sleep. But she wasn't sure how the Huntsmen had found them and wasn't willing to be caught unawares again. Maybe running had been a mistake. She didn't know what she was doing and she'd dragged Ryn along with her. She'd destroyed her phone and so left Cole and Jamie no way to contact her. Giving up Ryn had never been an option, but she might have made a mistake in not including her pack in her plans.

"Stop thinking." Ryn's voice cut through Kiara's storm of thoughts. "I can practically hear you."

Kiara gave a defensive shrug. "I don't know what else you want me to do."

"You don't have to *do* anything. Not right now." Ryn gestured at the bed behind Kiara. "I know you're tired. Get some sleep."

"The Huntsmen—" Kiara began.

"I'll stay up. I'll keep watch, or whatever." Ryn gave a wry grin. "We can take shifts. Very *Walking Dead*."

Kiara eyed the lumpy pillows. At any other time in her life she would have recoiled in disgust, but now they looked impossibly inviting.

"No one's going to come for us now, not so soon," Ryn pointed out. "We've got a few hours before we have to figure this out. Take the time. Sleep."

"If you're sure…"

"I am." Ryn stretched out on the chair and fished her phone from her pocket. "I've got Netflix on here. I'll be fine."

Kiara nodded. She would be able to think better after she had some rest. She crawled under the covers, pulled them up to her chin, and curled to face the wall. Ryn's measured breathing was soft at her back, and Kiara slowed her own to match. Within minutes, she was asleep.

WHEN KIARA WOKE, IT TOOK her a minute to remember where she was; the blank wall in front of her provided little in the way of clues. Then she registered the scratchy pillowcase under her cheek, and it all came back. She rolled onto her back and rubbed the sleep from her eyes.

"I thought you were going to sleep all day." At some point Ryn had joined Kiara on the bed and sat with her back propped against the headboard. The TV played soundlessly; closed captions scrolled across the bottom.

Having Ryn so close to her scrambled Kiara's brain. The bed was large enough that they weren't touching, but Kiara felt the warmth from Ryn's body. Though Kiara was sure she would regret it later, she gave in to impulse and rolled closer to rest her head in Ryn's lap.

Ryn didn't say anything, but skimmed her hand over Kiara's hair. Kiara leaned into the touch. Ryn's fingers carded through Kiara's hair, brushed across the shell of her ear, and sent shivers down her spine. Kiara wasn't sure who moved first, but Ryn bent down as Kiara arched up, and their lips met. The kiss was soft, hesitant, nothing like the one on the roof.

Kiara pushed herself up on her arms and twisted so that Ryn didn't have to bend so far. Ryn gathered Kiara's hair in gentle fistfuls and drew her in as her lips parted against Kiara's. The light touch of Ryn's tongue against Kiara's sparked heat, coaxed an ember to a flame. Kiara eased open Ryn's shirt buttons one by one until she could insert her hand, hold it flat against Ryn's chest, and feel the steady beat of Ryn's heart against her palm. Ryn's breathing hitched when Kiara slid her hand lower, cupped the gently rounded flesh of Ryn's breast, and drew her thumb delicately across the nipple.

Ryn's head dropped back against the headboard, baring her throat, and Kiara dragged her lips over the exposed flesh. Ryn tasted like sweat and warmth and citrus. Kiara nuzzled into the bend of Ryn's neck as her hands slid Ryn's shirt open. She wanted as much of Ryn's bare skin as she could get. Wanted it held so tightly against hers that when they finally parted, Kiara would carry part of Ryn with her.

Ryn leaned forward so Kiara could push her shirt down her arms, and once it was off Kiara tossed it to the side. Ryn cupped Kiara's face and brought her down for a kiss; her lips moved slow and sweet against Kiara's until Kiara whined helplessly. Her body was at once pliant and strung tight, as though without Ryn's touch she might snap in half, but until that promised touch came she was held in perfect, aching limbo.

Kiara allowed Ryn to ease her onto the bed, let Ryn pull her shirt off. When they were both topless, Ryn settled over Kiara, and Kiara gasped at the sensation of Ryn's skin, hot against hers. Her hands came up, wrapped around Ryn's back, and held her close. Ryn rocked against Kiara and moaned as their legs slotted together and Kiara's thigh hit just right.

Kiara felt drugged, drinking in the soft press of Ryn's skin sliding against her, as the golden, late-afternoon sunlight filtered weakly into the room. For the first time in days, months, years, the walls Kiara held so close and bricked up so tightly began to crumble.

Ryn brushed her lips down Kiara's neck and mouthed across her clavicle. The warmth of Ryn's bare skin was nothing compared to the wet heat of her open mouth, the drag of her tongue, and Kiara's hips rolled helplessly up into Ryn, to where her thigh rested between Kiara's legs.

"Tell me what you want," Ryn murmured against the curve of Kiara's breast before her tongue laved Kiara's hardened nipple. Kiara arched into it, and Ryn closed her mouth around Kiara's breast. Everything in Kiara's body tightened.

"You. I want you, Ryn."

Ryn's breath hitched with Kiara's admission, and her hands smoothed down Kiara's sides. Kiara writhed under the touch, then lifted her hips as Ryn tugged her leggings down.

"How do you want me?" Ryn's mouth drifted to Kiara's other breast, sucked until Kiara's eyes rolled back and she grabbed fistfuls of Ryn's hair to have something to hold onto.

"I want to feel all of you. I want you inside me. I want all of you."

Ryn pulled back, and Kiara let her hands fall to let Ryn look up at her. "You're sure?" she asked. Ryn's pupils were blown wide; the barest hint of her dark brown irises was visible.

Kiara nodded. Ryn surged in for another kiss, this one wetter, messier than the ones before, but still so achingly soft. They broke for air, and Ryn made her way down Kiara's body to drag Kiara's leggings from her legs. She dropped them to the floor behind her and returned to do the same to Kiara's panties.

Kiara parted her legs as Ryn slid between them. The rasp of Ryn's dress pants against the bare skin of her inner thighs sent shudders down her spine. Ryn hooked a hand into the bend of Kiara's knee, guided her leg back, and bared her entirely. Kiara bit her bottom lip; her cheeks heated as Ryn took her time looking down the length of Kiara's body.

"You're so beautiful like this." Ryn rubbed her thumb in gentle circles along Kiara's calf. "You always are." She flashed Kiara a rakish grin, then nipped at Kiara's ankle. "But like this, you're…" Her voice turned quiet, reverent. "So open. Exposed."

Kiara shuddered; her eyes closed. Ryn stroked from Kiara's breastbone to the thatch of curls between her legs, slid lower to part Kiara's slick folds and pressed one slim finger into her. Kiara's hands clenched around the sheets, her spine bowed when Ryn added a second finger, and she gave a desperate moan when Ryn leaned down and ran the flat of her tongue over Kiara's clit.

Ryn moved her fingers inside Kiara; her lips and tongue echoed the rhythm. The slow build of Kiara's orgasm sparked along her fingers, her toes, in a pulse that drew toward the center of her until she came, quaking, around the sensation of Ryn inside of her.

Ryn eased back, moved up Kiara's body, and delved into Kiara's mouth with her tongue. Kiara could taste herself, Ryn's lips slick with her, and she opened as wide as she could to draw Ryn farther in. Now it was Ryn's turn to whimper against Kiara's mouth as she rocked her thigh between Kiara's legs, the aftershocks from Kiara's orgasm rippling out until she could feel another build and roll over her.

"So good, you're so good," Ryn panted. She smoothed her hands over Kiara's forehead, cupped her face, and kissed her until they were both breathless.

Kiara worked a hand down between them, then wrenched away from Ryn's kiss long enough to confirm Ryn's preferences hadn't changed. "No penetration?"

Ryn nodded, the movements of her hips frantic now. Kiara fought with the button on Ryn's pants, swore, and then flicked it off—she'd sew it back on if she had to. She shoved her hand down, pressed the heel against Ryn's clit, and held onto Ryn's shoulder as Ryn rocked against her.

Ryn's breathing stuttered, broke against Kiara's skin in pants. Ryn's skin was damp with sweat under Kiara's other hand, where she held it against the base of Ryn's spine. Ryn's muscles flexed under Kiara's palm; the roll of her hips was sinuous as she worked toward her own orgasm. Ryn dropped her head, rested her forehead against Kiara's with her eyes screwed shut, and came with a sharp cry.

She fell, lax, against Kiara. Her chest heaved as she sucked in air; their hearts thundered against each other. Ryn took less than a moment to recover. She rose from Kiara and crossed the room on slightly unsteady legs until she reached her bag.

She rooted through it and returned with a small bottle of lube. Anticipation left Kiara's throat dry. She swallowed as Ryn settled onto the bed beside her. Ryn ran a reassuring hand down Kiara's flank. "Okay?"

Kiara nodded. Ryn dropped a kiss onto Kiara's knee and moved between Kiara's legs. Kiara had scooted to the edge of the mattress, and Ryn knelt on the floor in front of the bed. Kiara spread her legs wider as Ryn's hand moved down between them. She was wet from the first two orgasms, and Ryn sunk two fingers into her easily. The third took more coaxing, the push of it sparked bright along Kiara's spine. Ryn curled her fingers inside Kiara and rubbed against her g-spot. Kiara sucked in an uneven breath and flattened her hands against the bed.

Ryn's fingers continued to move, the cold touch of the lube eased between them until it warmed, and, with it, Ryn slowly added a fourth finger. The stretch was more intense now. Kiara's eyes fell shut; her breathing slowed as she concentrated on drawing air in as Ryn pushed into her.

Whereas her first orgasm had spread from her extremities in, this built differently. Pleasure radiated from her center in a low pulse that thrummed along her skin and in her blood as Ryn slicked more lube between them and slowly, unrelentingly, pressed more of herself into Kiara. Pain twined with pleasure; the ache of both stole Kiara's breath. Though she'd had plenty of sex, before and after Ryn, it never compared to this. Never came close to the dizzying intoxication of Ryn's hand inexorably working into Kiara's body, and the rush as her body complied.

"Come on, love, open up for me." Ryn coaxed. The cold touch of lube stole Kiara's breath; the sensation snapped along her senses and then was soothed when Ryn's tongue laved Kiara's clit. She sucked the heart of Kiara into her mouth as the fingers inside of Kiara twisted ever deeper.

The thickest part of Ryn's hand was against her now. Ryn's tongue swirled rapidly against Kiara's clit as the pressure mounted. Pain flared sharp, and Ryn instantly eased back, tongue soothing, before she pressed in again.

Kiara was ready for the pain this time, forced herself to relax and breathe, breathe, breathe through it. With one last push, Ryn was in.

Almost instantly the pain receded, replaced by an overwhelming feeling of fullness. Ryn twisted her wrist experimentally and sweat broke out over Kiara's skin. Her hands gripped the mattress, and her back arched fully. Pleasure swept through her so intensely that she thought she might fly apart from the force of it.

"Kiara, god," Ryn's voice was low, reverent. "You feel so good around me. Like hot, wet velvet. So soft and…" she trailed off as she moved her hand. Slowly at first, gentle twists. Then she pressed her mouth back to Kiara's clit and began to thrust her hand in earnest.

Kiara cried out, her eyes snapping shut as the onslaught of sensations crashed into her. She was oblivious to the mattress at her back, to the sheets seized in her clenched hands. She was exploding, she was flying apart, all of her was stars, and none of it would be contained.

As Kiara spiraled back to earth, her awareness of her body in the bed returned, and Ryn slowed. She guided Kiara's hand down, pressed it between Kiara's own legs so that she could feel Ryn's lube-slick wrist, feel where it disappeared into Kiara; Ryn's fist curled against her most intimate places.

Ryn kissed Kiara's inner thigh and gently eased her hand out of Kiara. The feeling of loss was instantaneous, and Kiara whined. Ryn grinned, slow and cocky, as she rose to her feet.

"Don't worry, love, I've got you." Ryn stroked down Kiara's side, teasing her nipple with fingers that were sticky with lube. Kiara arched into the touch, completely shameless.

"Don't stop, Ryn, please don't stop," Kiara begged.

"Hands and knees?" Ryn suggested. Kiara gave a full body shiver and nodded. She rolled over, her arms shaky, and moved farther up the bed before lifting herself up.

The mattress dipped as Ryn climbed up behind her. Ryn ran her hands down Kiara's sides and across the flare of Kiara's hips. She bent down and her hands moved to spread open Kiara's ass before her tongue stroked, hot and wet, over Kiara's puckered flesh.

Kiara jerked forward; a choked cry escaped her lips. They'd never done this. *Kiara* had never done this, but Ryn's tongue laved over her and Kiara rocked back into it before she knew what she was doing.

"Jesus, Ryn," Kiara moaned. Ryn hummed in response, and Kiara shuddered.

Ryn reached between Kiara's legs and circled the pad of her finger over Kiara's clit, drawing another fist-clenching orgasm from her.

As Kiara sagged forward, Ryn grabbed for the bottle of lube. She slicked more over her hand and rubbed it on Kiara's hot, swollen flesh.

Ryn slid back inside her, and the new angle sharpened the sensations; the intensity was so overwhelming that a sob broke from Kiara's chest.

Ryn stilled instantly. "You okay?"

"Don't stop." Kiara's voice was wet with tears. Ryn dropped a kiss to the base of Kiara's spine and pressed forward again. Kiara keened, a part of her shocked at the noise that came out of her, but unable to stop herself from making it again when Ryn pumped her fist.

Tears ran down her face and dampened the sheets below her. Her arms shook as she tried to hold herself up, keep herself still so that Ryn could continue to fuck her. Ryn grasped Kiara's shoulder, anchoring her in place. The grip steadied her, made a bruising counterpoint to the dizzying sensation of Ryn's fist moving in and out of her.

"So good for me, sweetheart, so good." Ryn's voice was thick. She stilled her wrist, but twisted her hand slowly inside of Kiara. Kiara rocked back against the sensation, against the feeling of so much of Ryn buried so deep in her. Ryn groaned and lifted her hand from Kiara's shoulder. Kiara heard a rustle of clothing and Ryn's sudden, sharp intake of breath, and knew that Ryn had slid that hand into her pants. Ryn's fist in Kiara resumed pumping, her movements were slow and gentle, and the mattress moved as Ryn rocked against her own fingers pressed against her clit.

Kiara shivered when Ryn's breathing quickened, the pace of it echoed in the movement of her fist. Despite Ryn's careful gentleness, Kiara felt every twist, every thrust, scrape through her as if all she was was one raw, open nerve. The pleasure mounted and mounted and mounted, thrummed through her so that Kiara couldn't do anything but weep with it. There was no crest or climax from orgasm, not with this, just an overpowering wash of sensation that rode the edge of *too much, too much, too much* and *please don't ever stop.*

Behind her, Ryn stiffened. Her hand inside Kiara shook slightly as she came, Kiara's spine bowed, and her forearms finally gave out.

"Love, love, love," Ryn murmured, breathless as she gently, so gently eased herself out of Kiara. "Oh, sweetheart." She helped Kiara turn to her side and pressed kisses over the tear tracks on Kiara's cheeks. "That was wonderful; that was so good. You did so well." She reached Kiara's lips and kissed her softly.

Ryn tasted like the lube, something chemical, but Kiara didn't mind. She wound her arms around Ryn's neck and pulled her closer, needing to feel Ryn's skin against her own.

They lay wrapped around each other until their heartbeats slowed to normal, and Kiara finally felt as though she'd returned completely to her own skin. Eventually though, the stickiness of the lube was too uncomfortable to ignore.

"Shower?" Kiara suggested.

"Yeah." Ryn agreed after a moment. "Probably a good idea." She kissed Kiara one last time and slid off the bed.

THE HOT WATER SOOTHED AWAY what was left of Kiara's tension from the fight that morning. She and Ryn showered together in relative silence, not needing to speak save to ask the other to pass the tiny bottle of shampoo. They wrapped themselves in the cheap, scratchy towels provided by the motel and curled onto the bed. Kiara snuggled close to Ryn.

It was hard to imagine how much had happened in the last few days: that suddenly everything had changed; that Ryn was back in her life now. It was harder still to imagine that it was the Huntsmen whom Kiara owed for that reunion. Why they were so focused on Ryn, Kiara couldn't imagine. She just knew she couldn't bear it if anything happened to her.

As though Ryn could tell the direction of Kiara's thoughts, she stroked light fingertips over Kiara's forehead, smoothing away the frown Kiara hadn't realized she was making.

Kiara closed her eyes against the sudden tightness in her throat and pressed closer.

The weekend had taken a toll. She'd never hurt anyone before, never injured a person, never caused harm deliberately. And she'd done so on two separate occasions now. Kiara wasn't sure what that said about her. It had been self-defense, each time, but violence was still violence. And the woman—the Huntress—was right when she'd accused werewolves of finding a thrill in it, of being dangerous. Kiara had caused more damage than a human would have. She'd *hurt* and even now wasn't sorry for it. She was sorry that she'd had to, but not sorry for having done what she'd needed to do to keep her pack safe.

The thought struck her, and she sat up so suddenly that Ryn stiffened in surprise.

"They're after you because you're lone. GNAAW can't—won't—" she corrected, "protect you because you're not with a pack."

"Yeah, and?" Ryn raised an expectant eyebrow.

"You don't have to be. You could join one. You could join ours." Kiara grabbed Ryn's hand and pressed it urgently between hers. "You'd be safe then. The Huntsmen would have to stop. GNAAW would make them."

Ryn pulled her hand free. "No," she said woodenly.

"Why not?" Kiara demanded. "It's not that big a sacrifice to make."

"Easy for you to say. You're not the one making it."

"We're not bad people." Kiara shook her head beseechingly. "I don't see how this is worse than the alternative."

"I'm saying no. I don't want to be a part of your father's pack. Don't ask me again."

"But I don't understand why you won't—"

"Exactly." Ryn cut her off. "You don't understand. You don't need to understand, but you do need to respect my decision."

Protests flew to the tip of her tongue, and it took all of Kiara's self-control to bite down on them and keep her mouth shut. All she wanted was for Ryn to be safe. It was hard to wrap her head around Ryn dismissing the only option Kiara could see. "Okay," she said finally, resigned, when she trusted herself to speak again. "We'll think of something else."

Ryn gave a curt nod, and slowly settled against the bed. It took a bit longer before she relaxed into Kiara, but eventually the tension drained from her body and her breathing evened out. Kiara wrapped an arm around Ryn's waist and snuggled in as close as she could. Ryn took Kiara's hand in hers, twining their fingers together against her bare chest, and soon they drifted off to sleep.

Chapter Twenty |

KIARA WASN'T SURE HOW MUCH time had passed when she woke up. The room was dark now, but in Vancouver in February that could mean it was anywhere from five-thirty in the morning to five-thirty in the evening. Kiara leaned across the bed to check the digital alarm clock on the bedside table, and saw that it was only six-forty at night.

Beside her, the bed shifted as Ryn rolled over onto her stomach. "Do you think this place has room service?" Her voice was muffled by the pillow.

Kiara hit the switch for the lamp. Illuminated by the warm glow of the lamp, as opposed to the harsh light of day, the room didn't look too bad. But then she remembered the sticky lobby floor and suppressed a shudder. "No. And if it did, would you want it?"

Ryn considered Kiara's point. "No, probably not."

It had been a long, exhausting day, though. Ryn was right; they should find something to eat. "Takeout?" she suggested.

"Sure." Ryn slipped out from the covers. Completely naked, she stretched, and Kiara watched helplessly, Ryn's skin limned gold by the lamplight. Ryn added an extra wriggle to her step as she crossed the room to her bag. She pulled out her phone and tossed it to Kiara.

"The passcode's 4247. In my contacts, there's a number for Chinese food. They make wicked sweet and sour pork." Ryn went into the bathroom.

Kiara unlocked the phone and refused to think about how many other nights she and Ryn had spent naked in bed, playfully fighting over the last piece of pineapple.

She scrolled through Ryn's contacts until she found the restaurant. Her thumb hovered over it. She had a lump in her throat. It was too much like before: sex-rumpled sheets, the lingering slickness of lube, Chinese food on its way.

A notification popped up onscreen: @VanCityStyle liked Ryn's photo on Instagram. Suddenly desperate for a distraction, Kiara tapped on it. The app opened up, and a picture of Ryn and Nathan filled the screen. He was grinning; his head was tilted to the side to display the flowers Ryn had created, and she stared out haughtily beside him. *Golden Afternoon with @TomeRader*. His kitchen was visible in the background.

Kiara's eyes flew to the date at the bottom: *One day ago*. This morning she hadn't had time to wonder how the Huntsmen had known where to find them, and after they'd escaped she'd been too exhausted to question it. But Ryn had made it too easy. Despite everything that had happened, she'd shared a picture of herself and Nathan, *in Nathan's apartment*, on social media. Kiara's fingers went numb around the phone.

"Can't you find the number?" Ryn came out of the bathroom, drying her hands on a towel, and gave Kiara a quizzical look.

"I found it," Kiara said shortly. Her chest felt tight. "I also found this." She turned the phone toward Ryn and displayed the screen.

Ryn frowned and crossed the room to get a better look. "My Instagram account?" she asked, raising an eyebrow. "Did you think I was hiding it from you or something? It's a public account."

"I know it's public." Kiara shoved the phone at Ryn and threw off the covers, no longer able to stay in the bed. "That's the problem."

Ryn stared at her, confusion warring with irritation on her face. "I'm a freelance hairstylist. This is how I get clients. Do you have a problem with that?"

"I have a problem," Kiara bit out as she yanked on her underwear, "with you publicly posting pictures of yourself in Nathan's apartment *when we're trying to hide you!*"

Ryn paled.

"Didn't you wonder how they found us this morning? How the Huntsmen knew to look at Nathan's? You led them right to us, Taryn. Right to us. You could have been killed. They could have taken you." Kiara pulled her pants over her hips, then shoved her tank top down over her arms. "Who knows what could have happened? And, god—" She broke into a joyless laugh. "Anyone could have walked in. We're lucky some soccer mom with a stroller didn't wander into that shitshow on her way to her minivan."

"I didn't think." Ryn sat woodenly on the edge of the bed, her phone forgotten in her hands. "I swear, Kiara, it didn't even occur to me."

"Well, it should have," Kiara snapped. "I don't want you to even think about touching your phone, do you understand? I'm doing everything I can to keep you safe, and if you're going to sabotage—"

"'Sabotage'?" Ryn rolled her eyes. "That's a little dramatic."

"Is it? You've been arguing with me about the best way to do this since Kings of Hearts."

"And, what, you thought I'd get my revenge by calling the Huntsmen up and saying 'Here I am, come get me'? For fuck's sake, Kiara." Ryn dropped her phone on the bedspread and stood with her hands clenched into fists at her sides. "What good would that have done me? Whose side do you think I'm on here?"

"You're not on mine, that's for sure." They were close now, nearly nose-to-nose, and Kiara hated that she was forced to look up just the slightest bit to meet Ryn's eyes. "You've been nothing but disrespectful this whole time. I'm the Alpha-designate of—"

"Of *not my pack*." Ryn's voice was the low growl of distant thunder. "You could be the Queen of England for all it matters to me. I don't care about whatever title you've taken—"

"Earned. I earned it. What have you earned, Taryn?"

"A life!" Ryn shouted. "I earned a life."

On the bedspread, Ryn's phone rang.

They both grabbed for it, but Kiara was quicker. For the second time that night, Nathan's face filled the screen. Kiara turned away from Ryn and swiped to answer.

"Nathan."

"Hey, K."

There was something off about Nathan's voice, and Kiara stilled. "What's going on?" she asked carefully. Ryn stepped into Kiara's line of sight, and whatever she saw on Kiara's face made the question she'd been about to ask die on her lips.

"I'm just at work—the library—doing some research. I think I found something about the Huntsmen. You and Taryn should come and take a look."

Kiara's mind raced. Something wasn't right. "Research, eh? You're turning into a regular Scooby."

Nathan laughed, and it rang hollow. "Yeah, you know me. But the thing is—" Kiara pressed her phone tighter to her ear. She could hear Nathan lick his lips nervously. "—there's sort of a time limit. Professor Ackbar needs the text I'm looking at for a seminar tomorrow morning. So I need you two to head down here now if you want to see it."

"I understand. We're on our way."

"Great. See you soon." The line went dead.

"Oh, cool, the library—what do you think he found?" Ryn asked curiously.

Kiara stared at her. "It's a trap."

Ryn frowned. "What makes you say that?"

"Professor *Ackbar*. Admiral Ackbar. 'It's a trap.'"

Ryn's face remained blank and uncomprehending.

"Ryn, we watched *Star Wars*."

"Was that the space one?"

Kiara gritted her teeth. "Never mind. Nathan's in trouble. We have to call Jamie and Cole. Oh, fuck." She rubbed a hand at the worried crease in her forehead and desperately wished for a cigarette. "Deanna is going to kill me."

"Was it the one with the space wizards?"

"Jedi, Ryn, they were *Jedi*."

THEY SHIFTED IN THE ALLEY behind the hotel. Kiara was prepared for it this time; she took her clothes off, folded them in a neat pile, and slid them under a nearby dumpster. There was no guarantee they'd be there when she got back, but there was no sense destroying another perfectly good outfit. Beside her, Ryn did the same.

They didn't have time to dawdle, or linger, but Kiara couldn't help but let her eyes drift over Ryn standing in the moonlight, clothed in nothing but a long fall of black hair. Ryn caught Kiara looking and stared back at her defiantly. Kiara dropped her gaze.

"He's at the university. It's a straight shot from here."

"As long as no one sees us."

"As long as no one sees us," Kiara agreed. There hadn't really been a discussion about how they were going to get there—a bus was out of the question, and there was no telling how long a cab would take. They could run it, though, as wolves.

From the street, a car honked and a man shouted angrily. Someone could come around the corner any second, and they'd certainly have questions about the two naked people.

As Ryn closed her eyes and drew in a deep breath—she always had needed a minute to center herself first—Kiara let the shift slide over her. Not the explosion of fur and fang of earlier that day, but a gentle, almost liquid transformation. Fur crawled over smooth skin, her face elongated, her ears moved from the sides to the top of her skull, and, when she dropped to all fours, padded feet and claws hit the concrete instead of hands.

Kiara shook herself, taking the time she hadn't been afforded in the parking garage to revel in the new shape. Her nostrils flared as she took in the scent of the city; her ears twitched with the onslaught of noise. Her limbs felt long and powerful and her muscles flexed in anticipation.

Ryn dropped to all fours; light-colored fur rippled as she shook herself.

It had been years since Kiara had been a wolf with anyone other than her own pack. She'd never had the experience with anyone but Ryn. Her body remembered what it was like, and her tail gave an eager wag as Kiara bumped her shoulder into Ryn's.

They'd done this in Edmonton: driven out of the city to some forgotten dirt road, just them and the wide open prairie, all blue sky and horizons. They'd run, flat-out, jumping fences, ditches.

Living in Vancouver, Kiara left the city with Cole and Jamie on occasion. It was exhilarating to run in both their forms, shift back and forth, and not have to worry about prying eyes or ears. Kiara enjoyed the city, appreciated what Vancouver had to offer, but a part of her would always yearn for the wide open freedom that she'd found on the prairie.

Well? Ryn tilted her head.

Kiara blinked away the memory. The long day with no food was beginning to wear on her, and she couldn't afford to keep sliding into distractions.

Let's go. She didn't wait for a response from Ryn, but trusted the other werewolf to follow.

It was just past seven, and, though the sun had set and the alleys were dark, a few people hurried through the evening. The pouring rain—would it ever let up?—kept most of them inside. The ones who were forced to venture out were huddled under umbrellas or kept their hooded heads down against the onslaught.

Kiara's coat protected her from most of the wet and chill. Her eyes squinted against the rain as she ran into it, but she used her other senses to help guide her. The way to the university was almost a straight line, and they could get there easily using the network of alleys.

Ryn ran to Kiara's left and just behind her, making it easy for the pair of them to keep to the edges of the alleys and stay in the shadows. Kiara hoped that the rain and their swiftness would be enough to convince anyone looking out that their eyes were playing tricks on them.

The gaps between the alleyways were the tricky part; for the second or so it took them to cross the road, they were bathed in the orange glow of the streetlights.

Despite the reason for their mad dash across the city, despite the rain, despite the words in the hotel that Kiara wished she could take back, that she wished Ryn could unhear, Kiara couldn't deny the thrill that coursed through her as she ran as she was meant to: not hiding, not downplaying her strength or her speed or the power in her body. She was letting it out and she wasn't doing it alone.

Werewolves generally preferred to live in packs because it felt better, having someone running alongside. It meant belonging. It meant safety. It meant strength.

They had moved out of the crowded main streets and into an area that was more residential. One-time single-family homes now housed two, or three, or sometimes four families crammed into converted apartments. The roads were quieter, and, as they continued, the houses got larger, the number of people inside smaller, until they wove through Point Grey and the wealth disparity became obscene.

Close to the university the houses vanished entirely, replaced with towering trees. The woods were one of Deanna and Arthur's favorite haunts, and where the showdown with crywolf had taken place last year.

Kiara's ears flicked back. There was movement to their right as Jamie and Cole snaked out of the trees to join them. Despite never having hunted together, the four wolves fanned out instinctually. Kiara remained point with Ryn on her left, Cole to her right, and Jamie taking up the rear.

Now the concrete had vanished and the wet soil made a soothing contrast. With the woods came a different set of obstacles; their path was less straight. They wove through the trees easily; their large bodies were sleek and graceful and made for this kind of terrain.

They matched, Kiara realized. They were gray wolves, all of them: Cole, the largest, had a coat that was thick and soft, dark slate-gray sprinkled with hints of white and tan; Jamie's brindled gray-brown fur paled to cream down her muzzle; Kiara's coat ran to silver, darkened at the tips and white underneath; Ryn was lightest in her pale white pelt with a gray stripe up her muzzle and forehead, which framed her ears and continued down her back to her tail.

They burst through the forest at the university proper.

You said Nathan is in the library. Jamie, how do we—

Hang on, Cole. Kiara slowed their loping run to a walk, making sure to keep them to the edges of the buildings. Cole bristled at her side. *We can't get into the building as wolves, and as humans we have the slight problem of being completely naked.*

Cole bared his teeth.

Good point, K. Jamie agreed. *If someone sees a bunch of naked people running around the university, they'll definitely call security.*

There's gotta be a bookstore, lockers, whatever. Let's just break in and grab what we need. Ryn kept a wary eye on Cole, who laid his ears flat against his head and growled.

Bookstore. Follow me. Jamie headed down a lane and they fell into line behind her.

Jamie led them around the back of the building that housed the bookstore. She ducked under the building's overhang and shifted to human. The wolves milled in front of her with their ears pricked to hear anyone making their way toward them. With a quick jerk, Jamie broke the lock, and then they were in.

"This way." Familiar with the layout, Jamie took them to the clothing section and grabbed sweatpants and hoodies—the easiest items to pull on—in whatever size might fit as the other three wolves shifted back to human.

Clothed now, and branded with the university's colors, they went to the door.

"We should probably grab the security tape on the way out of here, once we have Nathan," Jamie mentioned. "Or whichever security guard watches it is going to have a fit."

"Right. That's your job." Kiara decided. "Don't forget."

Jamie nodded. "And maybe leave some cash...?" She shrugged self-consciously when Ryn looked at her askance.

"What? It's my school. I don't want to like, *steal*."

"Hey!" Cole snapped. "I don't care about some overpriced sweats. We don't even know if Nathan's okay or if they..." He trailed off, rubbed an unsteady hand over his beard. "Can we just get him back?"

"We're going. I promise." Kiara gave his arm a squeeze. "Okay, here's what we know." She'd already discussed the details with them on the phone, but she went over the plan again. They couldn't afford to make mistakes, not when they weren't sure what the Huntsmen intended to do with Nathan.

"It's clearly a trap, Nathan gave us the heads up on that. So we know they have him. We don't know how many or what kind of weapons they have. Jamie, you're the most familiar with the library..."

"He's probably in his office, twelfth floor." Jamie nodded. "I can get us there. There's an elevator up, and two staircases on either end of the hall. His office is in the middle; they'll have to be spread out to guard each possible entrance."

"Okay, good." Kiara nodded approvingly. "They want Ryn; we want Nathan. I don't think they'll hurt him—"

"You don't know that! You're the one who said they threatened Deanna back at Kings of Hearts. We're wasting time!" Cole clenched his jaw.

"Calm down," Kiara commanded. "We're getting him. You hear me? We're going to get him. He's going to be all right."

"They want me." Ryn shrugged. "You said it. I'm here." She held out her arms. "So we'll give them me, and you'll get Nathan."

Kiara rolled her eyes in exasperation. "We're not giving you to them."

"I'll give me, then. I'm not going to be responsible for anyone getting hurt."

"No one is getting hurt and no one is giving themselves up. Come on." Jamie, ever the peacemaker, broke in.

"I'm just saying," Ryn argued. "This isn't your problem. I'm not your pack. You shouldn't be risking your lives for me. I won't let anyone else get hurt."

"Listen," Kiara ordered. "We're going to go up there. We are going to ask for Nathan. If they don't give him back, we are going to take him back."

"And what if there's more of them? What if it's not three, or four, what if there are six? A dozen?" Cole shook his head. "We're just going to say 'Please hand our librarian over,' and they're going to do it without question?"

"We can fight them, if we have to." The thought of it left a bad taste in Kiara's mouth; the memory of blood, thick and hot, coated her tongue. "But that's our last resort. They think we're violent—that 'lycanthropy' makes us that way, clouds our reason, our judgment. They're going to expect force and violence. They want us to react that way—so they can say we're threatening, that they acted in self-defense, that they started it. So we aren't going to give them that—not unless we have no other choice."

Cole dropped his head into his hands. "Again, so what are we going to do?"

Kiara swallowed. She'd been spinning the idea over in her mind since the call from Nathan. The idea would work, was possibly the only solution that would get them all home safe and sound, with no injuries to either side; but she wasn't sure if Jamie, Cole—and especially Ryn—would go with it.

"GNAAW has basically given The Huntsmen carte blanche with Ryn because she's not in a pack, and because she's not in a pack the Huntsmen think she's a danger."

"Right," Jamie agreed, patiently.

Ryn blew out an impatient breath. "I'm not joining your dad's pack."

"I know you're not, I know." Kiara took a deep breath. "But what if you joined mine?"

Chapter Twenty-One |

RYN FROWNED. "I DON'T UNDERSTAND."

Cole's head had snapped up; his honey-gold eyes were sharp on Kiara's.

"Oh, that's smart," Jamie approved. She elbowed Cole. "We're in. Obviously."

"Are you sure?" Kiara hid her nerves under a façade of calm. She was asking a lot from her cousin and her brother.

"Yes." Cole's answer was immediate this time. "Yes. Of course."

Kiara turned to Ryn. "This doesn't work without you. If you don't want to do this, if you really don't want to join a pack, we'll figure something else out." There was no question of leaving without Nathan. But Kiara knew in her heart that taking him back by force would mean blood spilled, and she wasn't sure whose it would be.

"It's not actually that hard to form a new pack," Jamie explained to Ryn, who continued to eye Kiara. "You need four adult wolves. One to stand as Alpha, and three who support them." She gestured to herself and Cole. "We're two. You'd be the third."

"And why do you get to be Alpha?" Ryn challenged Kiara.

Kiara lifted an eyebrow. "Do you want to do it?"

Ryn shook her head. "No, but what's going to make this pack any different than your dad's? Why should I agree?"

Kiara was prepared for Ryn's reluctance. "We form it, so we get to make the rules. We get to decide how it's run. GNAAW recognizes us. And the Huntsmen won't be able to come after you." It wasn't the perfect solution, but it was a solution. She hoped Ryn would see that.

"After tonight—" Kiara licked her dry lips. "If you don't want to stay, you don't have to. We won't ask anything from you. As long as I have your support, I'll stay Alpha, we'll have a pack that you'll be a member of. And you can go. You'll be under our protection, under GNAAW's protection, but not under our thumb."

"That's it?" Ryn asked suspiciously.

Cole nodded. "Beyond the basics—protect your pack, keep the secret, and don't hurt anyone—packs are free to have as many or as few internal rules as they'd like. Some of the larger packs pay a tithe. Some all live together. Some are scattered. It's up to the Alpha to decide how it's run."

"I won't ask you to do anything you're not comfortable with. I won't ask you to do anything. Except for this," Kiara said haltingly. "We need to get Nathan, and we need to make sure you're protected. This—" She gestured at the four of them. "—this accomplishes both of those things."

Ryn closed her eyes. "Give me a minute."

Cole made a bitten-off noise of frustration and glanced toward the library.

"Just—a minute. Give her a minute." Kiara insisted.

Ryn had stepped away from the group. She stared out into the rain with her arms wrapped around herself in the oversized hoodie.

Impatience clawed at Kiara's throat. Jamie took her hand. She squeezed it.

Kiara wasn't sure if she was doing the right thing. She didn't know how she was going to tell her father. She didn't know what her choice would mean for his pack—her, possibly, former pack. She closed her eyes and gripped Jamie's hand tighter.

Ryn turned around. "Okay. I'll do it."

Relief weakened Kiara's knees. "Thank you."

Cole pulled Ryn into a hug. He lifted her off her feet, and she yelped. "Welcome home," he said.

Ryn wriggled free, but Kiara didn't miss the flush on her cheeks. "Whatever, man. Let's go get Mowgli, shall we?"

THE LIBRARY WAS ONE OF the biggest buildings on campus. Though it wasn't very late, the building was nearly deserted. It closed to students and the general public at six o'clock, so the only people still there would be working. Kiara glanced up, shielding her eyes from the rain. A few lights twinkled, one on the twelfth floor that she thought might be Nathan's.

"Right, so how are we going to do this?" Ryn asked. For the first time since they'd fled Nathan's that morning, she looked nervous tugging on the sleeves of her sweater.

"Quickly and quietly," Kiara advised. "Remember what I said—we can't give them any excuse. We'll be calm and polite and then we'll get the hell out of here."

As she had with the bookstore, Jamie led them around the back and through a fire exit.

"Elevator, not the stairs," Kiara decided. "We have to stay together. And look as nonthreatening as possible," she said pointedly to Cole, whose bearded jaw was firmly set and whose hands were clenched into large fists.

Cole scowled, but relaxed his hands as Jamie hit the button for the elevator.

The ride to the twelfth floor was excruciating. The nervous tension the wolves felt overwhelmed the small space, and Kiara could feel it crawling over her skin. It was as if they were walking into the wolves' den. *Or did one walk into the lion's den? Whichever. They weren't the ones lying in wait. Lion-in-wait. Did that mean it was lions?*

"Get a grip," she muttered to herself.

"What?" Jamie asked, her voice shockingly loud in the small space.

"Nothing. Just. Let me do the talking." Kiara swallowed hard as the elevator dinged to a stop. She squared her shoulders and settled her face into her most neutral expression as the doors slid open.

A man stood across from the elevator and he had a gun—*Why did they have so many guns? Didn't they know this was Canada?*—leveled at them. His serious expression faltered and then broke into a laugh.

Kiara's neutral expression hardened as she struggled not to scowl. "Is there a problem?"

"You just—ooh boy," he wheezed in a southern drawl as his gun wavered. "You guys look like a weird sports team. I just mean—you're lycans, right? Like. I expected leather jackets and maybe a biker chain. Not—" he broke down, chuckling. "You're all in sweatpants!"

Kiara exhaled slowly through her nose. Laughter wasn't the welcome she'd expected, but it was better than a fight. She glanced at the rest of her pack and supposed that they did look ridiculous.

"I mean, I get it," the Huntsman continued as he visibly tried to pull himself together. "Your clothes don't come along when you change, but I gotta say, you'd've looked more badass showing up naked."

"Duly noted," Kiara said dryly. Behind her, Cole vibrated. "If we can move past our appearance, could we please speak to whomever is in charge?"

"Right." He straightened and leveled the gun again. "Sorry." With his gun-free hand, he hit the comm button on his bulletproof vest.

"Ma'am, I've got four lycans at the elevator bank."

The comm crackled with the Huntress's voice. "Is the lone one there?"

Ryn stepped out from behind Kiara and raised her middle finger at the comm.

"Yes, ma'am."

"Send them down, Joel."

The Huntsman gestured with his gun, and they headed down the hallway.

"Remember," Kiara warned in a low voice, "no matter what they say or do, do not do anything that can be construed as aggressive. We do not want to give them an excuse."

Jamie and Ryn murmured in agreement. Cole said nothing, and Kiara shot him a warning look.

"This one is Nathan's." Jamie stopped them. Unlike the other offices, this one had its door wide open. Kiara's brow furrowed. She couldn't hear anyone in the room. Cole pushed past her and was inside before she could tell him not to go in.

"It's empty," he snarled.

Kiara stuck her head in. She wasn't sure what she expected to see—books pulled off the shelves, his computer smashed—but with the exception of the desk chair spilled onto its side, nothing appeared to have been disturbed. That, somehow, made her more uneasy.

"Keep walking. Please." Joel from the elevator had followed them and pointed to the large conference room at the end of the hallway.

The silhouettes of four standing people were evident through the large glass window, with a fifth who was seated in a chair at the table. She could tell from his posture that it was Nathan, and the fury that she'd managed to keep in check all evening bloomed hot in her chest.

Cole started down the hallway. Kiara should have called for him to wait, but decided against it. He was smart enough not to do anything stupid. Probably.

A man opened the door as they neared. He held an assault rifle casually in one hand. Cole ignored him and walked past, Jamie and then Ryn followed, and Kiara brought up the rear.

Joel followed, closed the door behind them, and stood in front of it.

There was an angry red bruise on Nathan's cheek, and his broken glasses sat on the table in front of him. He squinted, and Kiara knew his vision was bad enough without his glasses that he had trouble seeing who they were.

Cole growled, low and vicious, and Nathan rolled his eyes. "Seriously? When someone tells you it's a trap you're not supposed to walk into it."

Another man stood behind Nathan and rapped him across the back of his head. "You warned them?"

Nathan winced and rubbed at the spot.

"Professor Ackbar, really, Sandeep? Mr. Roberts wasn't exactly subtle." The Huntress stepped forward. Her hand rested casually on a Taser as she watched Cole, whose eyes were rapidly draining of color.

"No one touches him again."

"Oh, this?" Gingerly, Nathan touched his cheek. "It's nothing. A scratch. You should see the other guy."

The Huntress looked down at Nathan and arched a perfectly shaped eyebrow. He swallowed, snapped his mouth shut, and sank into his chair.

"What's your play here?" Kiara asked the Huntress. "I don't think you'll really hurt Nathan—not when your whole mandate is to protect humans."

"Sacrifices can be made if necessary." Her hand fell onto Nathan's shoulder and tightened until he flinched. "But I don't think we'll need to go that far. I know GNAAW has told you to hand the lone one over. If you disobey them, it won't just be us who will hunt you down."

"There won't be any more need for hunting." Kiara stepped back until she stood side by side with Ryn. She clapped her hand to the side of Ryn's neck. "She's pack now." Ryn's pulse beat steadily under her palm; something electric sparked between their skins.

"You can't do that," Sandeep spoke up. "You're not the Alpha, you can't add members to your pack. We've done our research."

"Things have changed." Cole moved to Kiara's side. She lifted her hand from Ryn's neck and laid it on his. Jamie stepped up next, neck bared, and allowed Kiara to do the same to hers.

"We're pack now. The four of us. Ryn isn't lone, and you cannot have her." Kiara dropped her hand from Jamie's neck, and when she turned back to the Huntress she knew her eyes had gone stormy gray. "Now, give us Nathan."

The Huntress's eyes flicked between them; clearly she was no longer certain. "GNAAW doesn't know about this."

"GNAAW will. You can't touch us now."

A ghost of a smile flitted across the Huntress's face. "Your faith in that organization is… endearing."

"What's that supposed to mean?" Ryn spoke up before Kiara could stop her.

The Huntress shrugged gracefully. "They're the ones who brought you to our attention. They sent us your location, your details. A lycan named Davis said they'd been having trouble here with the lone ones lately, that they needed someone to clean up before there was an incident like the one last year."

"GNAAW sent you to the club?"

"Davis has been feeding us details on the lone ones for months. He sent us there and then to your friend Mr. Roberts's apartment. He was adamant we take care of your new packmate for him." The Huntress shrugged and stepped away from Nathan.

"I see." Kiara wasn't sure what to do with that information. She had no idea how to process the knowledge that the GNAAW rep had directed the Huntsmen right to them.

It didn't matter, not right now. Right now she needed to get her pack out of here, and that included Nathan. "Get up," she ordered him. "We're leaving."

Nathan eased out of the chair with one eye on the man standing behind him as though he expected to be shoved back into it. When Sandeep didn't move, Nathan scooped up his glasses and edged around the table. Jamie grabbed his hand and pulled him into the middle of the pack. Cole stepped directly in front of Nathan, hiding him as much as he could, though Nathan was nearly a head taller.

"We're done here then?" Kiara wanted confirmation from the woman that this was over.

"For now," the Huntress agreed. "Keep your pack under control and you won't see us again. But if you don't…"

"Well, hang on now." Joel spoke up from the back. "I don't see how this changes much. I mean, y'all can't just magic a pack into existence, can you? That doesn't seem very—" He sucked his teeth. "—sporting."

"Joel." The edge to the Huntress's voice was sharp.

"Now, ma'am, I think we need to consider this further. I mean, is this new pack GNAAW registered? Are they complyin' with all the regulations? Cause from where I'm standing,"—between them and the door—"it seems like, instead of a brand new pack, we've just found ourselves three additional targets. Me 'n some of the boys have been talking, and we think maybe it's time our understanding with GNAAW came to an end. These critters are dangerous, and where I come from, you don't reason with something that might eat you. You just make sure you kill it first." He pointed his gun at the center of Kiara's chest.

Chapter Twenty-Two

KIARA LET OUT A SLOW, even breath. If the bullets in Joel's gun were silver—and she had no doubt that they were—he could inflict serious damage, maybe death.

Nathan laughed. "Okay, for starters, you're in a room with four fully grown werewolves. With one exit. That you're standing in front of. Do you really think there's any chance of you doing this and leaving here alive?" He snorted. "Yeah, you'd probably get one good shot off. But then you've got three pissed-off, fully grown werewolves who are avenging their Alpha. You think that ends well? You think that ends with you on top?" He shook his head and pushed past Cole to stand side by side with Kiara. "And let's imagine that it does—how are you going to explain a shootout in the library? And a dead librarian?"

Kiara caught Cole's flinch out of the corner of her eye.

"We have resources." Joel's mouth twitched with irritation. "We'd clean it up."

"*I* have resources," the Huntress said. "Stand down, Joel."

"No." His eyes darted past her, seeking backup from the two other Huntsmen. Sandeep shook his head, and the third man remained silent. "No," Joel insisted. "We can't make deals with 'em. They aren't human. They're rabid and they need to be put down."

"You know our mandate, Joel. We seek a cure, not a kill."

"We're not diseased," Ryn snarled. "We don't need—"

"Not the time," Kiara commanded.

Jamie placed her hand on Ryn's shoulder to keep her in place. Ryn would hate being ordered to shut up, but Kiara had to demonstrate that she would be obeyed by her new pack and especially by Ryn.

"Stand down," the Huntress repeated.

"Fuck it." Joel's pulse spiked, and Kiara sprang forward. He pulled the trigger as she knocked his arm up. The bullet plowed into the ceiling, and Kiara and Joel crashed to the floor. He struggled under her, but his size was no match for her inhuman strength. She grabbed his arm that held the gun and dug in her fingers until she could feel the blood under her nails. He swung a fist at her, and she didn't so much as rock when it connected with her cheek.

Kiara's pack had formed a solid line between the Huntsmen and Kiara. With a hand against his chest, Cole pinned Nathan to the far wall out of the line of fire as Nathan squawked in indignation. Cole ignored him and growled low and steady at the Huntsmen.

"Drop the gun or I tear off your hand." Kiara tightened her grip on Joel, and he paled.

"I'll let her do it, Joel." The Huntress shook her head at her two other men, who'd trained their weapons on the other werewolves. Slowly, they lowered their guns.

Joel swore, but dropped the gun.

"Jamie."

Kiara's cousin obeyed immediately. She picked up the gun by the butt and set it on the boardroom table.

"I'm going to get up, and we are going to leave. And *you* are going to stay down." Kiara stared at the man on the ground before her. He met her stormy gray eyes with a hard stare of his own, but gave a short jerk of his head in response.

Carefully, Kiara rose. No one else moved.

"Are we done here?" she asked the Huntress for the second time. The woman nodded; her lips were thinned into a hard line that promised Joel's day wasn't going to improve.

"Good. Let's go."

She turned, went out the door, and took an immediate left to the staircase, ignoring the elevator farther down the hall.

Nathan was close on her heels, Ryn behind him, and Jamie behind her with Cole at their backs. She didn't speak as they clattered down the stairs; her ears were pricked for sounds of the Huntsmen following them. When Nathan tried to say something, Jamie hushed him, and his irritated silence accompanied them the rest of the way down.

In the lobby of the library, Nathan shoved to the front. He pulled the ID card from the clip on his jeans and swiped the keypad to unlock the front door.

"Do I want to know how you got in here?" he asked.

"No," Kiara responded.

Tires screeched as a car share rounded the corner and skidded to a stop in front of them. Deanna shut down the car and flung herself out of it.

"Ohmygod." She dropped an overflowing purple backpack to the ground and threw herself at Nathan, who staggered under her weight. "Oh, man. Oh, boy. Oh, wow! I got here as soon as I could." She pressed her face into the side of his neck as he held her close. "I'm so glad you're okay." She finally pulled herself off of him. "I am so glad that the rest of you aren't naked." She nudged the backpack with her toes, and it fell over, spilling out a jumble of clothes. "I was really worried you'd all be naked."

"*That's* what you were worried about?" Nathan asked.

"Well, like, and that you'd be murdered by some psycho werewolf hunters but, yeah, I was worried about the naked part." Deanna bit her lip and somehow managed to look adorably sheepish. "I kind of knew everyone would save you, though. They're good at that." She met

Kiara's eyes and smiled. "And this is, like, Cole's second time saving your ass, so—"

"So let's not make it a third," Kiara said pointedly.

"Right! Everyone in." Deanna gestured at the car.

"Hang on—" Jamie rubbed a hand over the back of her neck. "Babe… do you have any cash? We, uh, kinda owe the bookstore. And I have to pick up some security tapes."

Deanna looked as though she was about to ask, but just shook her head. She reached into her purse, took out her wallet, and pulled out a handful of bills. "I don't know if this is enough, but—"

"It'll do," Kiara decided. "Jamie, you'll destroy the tapes and meet us at your place?"

Jamie nodded. She planted a quick kiss on Deanna's lips, then jogged off toward the bookstore.

Cole had already opened the car's rear door and ushered in Nathan, who grumbled, "I said 'shotgun.'"

Deanna picked up her backpack and tossed it into the footwell of the passenger seat as she dropped into the driver's. Ryn smiled sweetly at Kiara. "You're smaller," she said.

"I'm the Alpha," Kiara countered.

"The small Alpha."

A muscle in Kiara's jaw twitched, but she didn't want to give the Huntsmen any more time to change their minds about letting Ryn go, or for Joel to convince them they were all a threat. Without a word, she crawled into the backseat and forced Cole to move into the middle. He didn't seem to mind, and had an arm around Nathan before Kiara found her seatbelt.

☾

"ALL RIGHT, LET ME GET this straight." Deanna paced the carpeted floor of her and Jamie's living room. "The GNAAW rep was the one who tipped the Huntsmen off in the first place? And not just about Ryn at the club, or that she existed, but that we were at Nathan's? How did he even know about that?"

Kiara shrugged, her mouth full of bagel. She hadn't eaten since breakfast that morning, and all Deanna and Jamie had in the fridge that was easy to make was bagels and cream cheese. This was Kiara's fourth bagel, and she was strongly considering a fifth.

"You've all got phones, right?" Nathan sprawled across the carpet, one hand flung over his relatively useless eyes and Arthur's head propped lovingly on his stomach. "Maybe they're tracking your phones."

"That's like some NSA shit," Ryn remarked. "Is that even legal?"

Deanna stopped her pacing and stared incredulously at Ryn. "Are werewolves?"

"Good point," Ryn allowed.

"Speaking of." Nathan raised himself up on his elbows. "How are you gonna register your new pack? Is there a form you have to fill out?"

"New pack?" Deanna dropped to sit beside Kiara on the couch. "What does he mean, new pack?"

"Well." Cole finished spreading cream cheese on a bagel half. "We kind of made a new one. Or Kiara did. And the rest of us joined." He gestured with the bagel to encompass Kiara and Ryn as well as himself.

"You're, ah," Kiara paused, not sure how to say it. "You're kind of still part of our dad's pack."

"I'm what?" Deanna squeaked. "I'm not part of a pack!"

Cole winced. "Kind of, you are. We weren't—I mean—it's not like—it's a bit different when you're a human."

"Like no one actually tells you?"

Kiara nodded. "I mean, we thought Jamie…"

"Jamie what?" Jamie unlocked the front door and stepped through. She was wearing her own clothes and carried a small bag that she tossed to Cole. Evidently she'd picked up their clothes from where they'd stashed them before shifting.

"Apparently," Deanna said, ice in her voice, "I'm part of a werewolf pack."

"Oh. Um. Yes."

Deanna glowered.

"It didn't seem like a big deal?" Jamie offered. She shot Kiara a murderous glance. "It's not really a thing, and only some people ascribe significance to it. But, um, yeah. My uncle kind of… added you."

"Your uncle added me to your pack, and you didn't bother to tell me?" Deanna's voice rose, as did her eyebrows.

Jamie winced. "It was kind of presumptuous on his part. I mean, we weren't even living together. And I wasn't going to say anything because it wasn't really a big deal."

"Except now we're a part of different packs?!"

"Uhhh… yes. That's also new." Jamie sent a beseeching glance to Kiara.

"For the love of…" Kiara rolled her eyes. "Do you want to join my pack?"

"Obviously."

"Okay, come here." She beckoned Deanna over and licked the cream cheese off her fingers before slapping her hand to the side of Deanna's neck. Deanna blinked and looked at Kiara expectantly.

"What?" Kiara said, withdrawing her hand. "That's it. It's not like a naked, howl at the moon, blood-sisters ritual."

Deanna looked disappointed. "That's uninspired."

"You're uninspired," Kiara shot back, offended.

"Well, you're the loser who just added an uninspired person to your pack, so that means you're *double*—"

"How about we get GNAAW on the phone," Cole interrupted.

"Why would we do that?" Ryn asked. "From literally every interaction we've had with them this week, I think it's pretty clear that they can't be trusted."

Nathan sat up, dislodging Arthur. "We've—well, you've—only talked to that Davis guy, right? It's just been him?"

Kiara nodded.

"Maybe it's not GNAAW as a whole, then. Maybe just that guy." He shrugged. "Let's go over his head."

Kiara thought about it as she washed down her bagel with a glass of milk. "All right," she decided.

"You can use my phone, Alpha," Deanna said with a wink and tossed it to Kiara.

Chapter Twenty-Three |

"THIS IS RIDICULOUS," KIARA GROUSED. "What kind of emergency line has someone on hold for," she checked the clock on the oven, "twenty-three minutes?"

"Apparently that happens sometimes with 911. I bet the werewolf emergency line has a smaller staff, so it's really not that surprising."

"Shut up, Nathan." Kiara glanced into the living room to make sure that the rest of the pack and Nathan, who couldn't see the screen but seemed content to lie with his head in Cole's lap and listen, were thoroughly engrossed in *Captain America: Civil War*. She got up from the kitchen table. She silently eased open the freezer and took the pack of cigarettes she'd stashed there the last time she'd dog sat.

"I'm going out for some air," she announced, having tucked the cigarettes in the pocket of the university hoodie. No one bothered to turn around.

Kiara stuffed her feet into a pair of Deanna's flats and left. She was glad that Deanna had suggested she use the headset with the phone—no way she'd have held it up to her ear for as long as she'd had to wait. And her hands were free, which was perfect, she thought as she jogged down the stairs and pushed out into the street.

The downpour had stopped. Kiara tapped a cigarette free from the pack and lifted it to her lips before she reached into the hoodie's pocket and fished around for the—

"Shit."

"Forget something?" Ryn appeared behind her and held out a lighter. Kiara sighed and took it from her.

"Thank you." She pulled out one of the earbuds.

"No problem." Ryn lifted her hands up and stretched, groaning. "It's good to get out. No offense to your friends—our friends, whatever—and the change of scenery is nice, but I'm sick of being in a room with five other people and a dog for the fourth day in a row."

Kiara nodded and toyed with the lighter. "Are you okay?"

Ryn shrugged. "I don't know, exactly." She bent, touched her toes. "I don't know what to make of this whole 'pack' thing."

"You don't have to make anything of it." Kiara scuffed her shoe against the sidewalk and tried not to let Ryn see how nervous she was. "It doesn't have to mean anything—not if you don't want it to."

Ryn turned her head to look at Kiara. "What if I want it to mean something?" she asked softly.

A flicker of hope replaced the knot that had existed in Kiara's chest since the moment she'd seen Ryn on that stage. "Do you?"

"Yeah." Ryn straightened and moved toward Kiara. "You left your pack for me. Your family. That's gotta mean something, right?"

"Well." Kiara swallowed, her mouth going dry. "Jamie and Cole came with me, so I didn't really leave—"

"You did." Ryn took Kiara's hand, laced their fingers together. "And this new pack—we can build it ourselves, right? Make it what we want it to be?"

Kiara nodded, unable to take her eyes away from their joined hands. It was ridiculous, really. Hours before—had it only been that?—they'd been as close as two people could be. But somehow that closeness paled in comparison to what she was feeling now. Her chest ached as the love she'd never stopped feeling for Ryn slowly escaped the vault she'd locked it in.

"Then let's make it a good one. And get it off to a good start." Ryn lowered her head, and Kiara tilted up her chin, and the kiss when their lips met was so soft that Kiara thought they might just be melting together.

They were slammed apart. The force was enough that Kiara crashed onto the sidewalk with the breath driven from her lungs. She lay there, stunned, and gasped for air. Her forearms stung, their flesh skinned bloody, but she could already feel them healing. It took longer, an eternity, before she was able to draw in a breath, and when it finally hit she rolled over to her side, coughing so hard tears spilled down her cheeks.

Ryn had been thrown to the ground as well, and when Kiara lifted her head she saw Ryn pinned down while a brown werewolf, his fur grizzled white around his muzzle, snapped viciously at her throat. Ryn had her hands around his neck, and her forearms shook as she tried to hold him back.

Kiara didn't bother to shift. She was on her feet in one fluid motion and dug her hands into the thick ruff on the wolf's neck. He snarled and twisted his head toward her as she hauled him off of Ryn. He was three times her size, and his weight far exceeded Kiara's, but she had no trouble throwing him against the side of the building.

He was on his feet again in a second. Ryn struggled to hers, and Kiara placed herself in front of Ryn.

Quit protecting her. His ice-blue eyes gleamed in the darkness.

"She's mine to protect." Power coursed through Kiara and the promise of terrifying strength itched in her gums and tingled in the tips of her fingers.

She's dangerous. The lone ones are going to bring us down. They put us at risk. He wove in front of them, holding them at bay and away from the building's door.

"*You're* putting us at risk right now. Anyone could see you." Ryn stepped up beside Kiara. She balanced on the balls of her feet and lowered into a crouch.

His hackles rose, and bared teeth gleamed in the streetlight. *This is your last chance, girl. Either you let me have her, or you go down with her.*

Kiara's laugh was a knife-edge. "Oh, I don't think we'll be the ones going down."

He let out a furious growl and charged for her. His mouth wide, his breath hot and wet against her face, she swung a clenched fist against the side of his muzzle. Fangs broke with the impact. The skin on her knuckles split as she grabbed for his throat with her other hand. He snarled and twisted out of her grip before he turned on a dime and lunged at Ryn.

Ryn was ready. She spun and kicked him full in the face; her blow landed in the same place as Kiara's. This time when he fell it was with a high-pitched whine; blood dripped from his mouth and none of it theirs.

"Give it up, old man." Kiara's hand had already healed. His teeth probably wouldn't.

Give her up.

"You missed a memo," Kiara taunted. The longer this went on, the more certain she was that Davis was acting without GNAAW approval. The organization would never sanction an attack as a werewolf in the middle of the city—not even on a street like Deanna and Jamie's, which was relatively quiet. "Are they not keeping you in the loop like they used to?"

There obviously hadn't been time to talk to GNAAW, to let them know about Kiara's new pack, but Davis didn't have to know that.

His nose wrinkled, his growl deepened as he flattened his ears against his head and angled toward Ryn again.

"She's not a lone wolf anymore; she's pack now, asshole. My pack."

You don't have a pack. His disdain was obvious. *You need four. I only see two.* He gathered himself, his muscles bunched under his thick brown pelt.

"I guess we could go back inside." Cole stood at the top of the building's front steps. Jamie was silhouetted in the light from the lobby behind him and had her phone in her hand, filming. "But I think GNAAW is going to be interested in the footage we can show them."

You're children. You have no right.

Kiara decided she'd had enough of Davis. "I have every right." She leapt forward and locked her arms around his throat. He struggled under her, tried to buck her off and then roll. She held fast, tightened her grip until she could feel the frantic beat of his heart slow. It took longer than she would have liked, but eventually his legs gave out and he dropped to the ground. She held on, making sure he was really unconscious, before she released him and stood.

"Dude." Jamie shook her head. "What the hell?"

The phone, which Kiara had lost when Davis crashed into them, suddenly ceased blaring its tinny hold music from the speakers.

"Thank you for your patience. This is the GNAAW emergency line. Mallory speaking—how may I help you?"

"You wanna grab that?" Kiara asked Cole. He nodded and hurried down the steps.

"Hi, Mallory," he said, turning away. "This is Cole Lyons here in Vancouver, and we've got a bit of a situation with one of your reps…"

"What do we do with him now?" Ryn kicked, none-too-gently, at Davis' side. He'd slowly reverted to his human form, and lay sprawled naked on the concrete. "We're sort of… conspicuous."

Kiara rubbed the back of her neck. "I don't know. I've only been the Alpha for three hours. Give me a bit of time to adjust."

Jamie tucked her phone in her pants and jogged down the stairs. "The boiler room in this building is in the basement and solid concrete with a steel door. We can stick him in there until GNAAW can come get him, assuming that's within the next few hours."

"Somehow I think they'll want this cleaned up ASAP."

It took three of them to haul Davis downstairs. Each them could have carried his weight on their own, but none of them were particularly excited about having to drape his naked body over their backs.

"Seriously, though, you get that this is embarrassing." Nathan had come downstairs and volunteered to hold the doors open. He was still squinty-eyed without his glasses, but seemed to have no qualms about mocking them for what he could see.

"Do you want to help carry?" Ryn asked. She held one of Davis' legs as far in front of her as she could. Jamie had picked up his other leg, and Kiara held his wrists as they maneuvered him down the staircase.

"You look like you've got it." Nathan pressed against the concrete wall as they passed him. "Do we have an ETA on the actual, official GNAAW folks, or is Deanna going to have an angry, naked man in her basement for the rest of the night?"

"It's my basement, too." They made it into the boiler room, and Jamie dropped the rep to the ground with zero regard for his comfort.

"Also, isn't he going to wake up? That magical healing thing isn't going to kick in any second?"

Kiara shrugged. "We'll just knock him out again." Though Nathan did have a point—she'd been planning to leave Davis there and simply lock the door, but if he did wake up before GNAAW arrived, it was unlikely that he'd just sit quietly and wait to be picked up by the werewolf authorities. And she did not want to have to explain to Jamie and Deanna's neighbors why a screaming, naked man was locked in their boiler room

Jamie looked at her, and Kiara sighed. "Fine, all right? I'll stay with him." GNAAW had better get here soon.

"I'll stay too."

Kiara looked at Ryn with surprise.

"What?" Ryn shrugged. "I don't trust this asshole not to pull some more shit. And yeah, yeah—" she cut off Kiara's protest before Kiara had fully formed it, "I know you could deal with him yourself. But you don't have to. So I'll stay."

"Great!" Nathan clapped his hands. "Sounds like an A-plus plan. Now that everything here has been sorted out, I'm going to have your handsome brother escort me home. As you may have noticed—" He gestured at his face. "I'm in need of a Seeing Eye dog."

"Cole's going to love being called that," Kiara said dryly. "Maybe pick a better term."

"Oh, no, I wanna see his face." Jamie snickered and ushered Nathan out the door.

"So." Kiara sat with her back against the closed door.

"So," Ryn agreed. She slid down the wall and tucked her feet under Kiara's thigh.

Kiara picked at her chipped nail polish. "You don't have to date me." The words left a chalky aftertaste. "I mean, to be in my pack or whatever. I don't want you to feel like that's part of the deal. Because it isn't. You can not date me. You can date other people. You don't have to do anything... you don't have to earn my protection. I want to be clear about that." She was pretty sure that Ryn's kiss outside hadn't been coerced, or from a sense of obligation, but she needed to be certain.

"Okay." Ryn nodded. "Thank you for saying that."

Kiara swallowed and picked off another flake of polish. She'd respect Ryn's choice.

"But if I want to date you...?" Ryn leaned forward. "What if." She licked her lips in an uncharacteristic show of nervousness. "What if I wanted to try again?"

Kiara fought against the swell of hope in her chest; every instinct urged her against a display of emotion and vulnerability. Except—that had been the problem the first time around. She'd expected Ryn to be able to read her mind, to know how Kiara felt even when Kiara refused over and over again to demonstrate it. She'd loved Ryn, loved her with her whole heart and soul, but hadn't been able to say so, not explicitly.

If they were going to try again, really try, Kiara was going to have to get over herself and her hang-ups and make a real effort to communicate. She owed it to Ryn and she owed it to herself.

Her silence must have gone on too long, because Ryn drew her feet back, pulled her knees up to her chest, and wrapped her arm around them. "I'm sorry," she said awkwardly. "It's fine if you don't want that."

"No." Kiara gripped Ryn's hand. "I do, I do want that. I really want it, Ryn. I've wanted it since I saw you at Kings of Hearts. Hell," she broke off into a laugh that was dangerously watery. "I've wanted that since I left you in the first place."

"I thought you'd come back," Ryn confessed. "I didn't leave the apartment for three days. I was so sure you'd stomp back in any minute, and I didn't want to miss you when you did."

Kiara dropped her forehead on top of their joined hands. "I almost did. I smoked a whole pack of cigarettes out on the front step that second day, trying to get up the nerve to go inside. But I just... I was dumb, it was dumb, but I couldn't bear to admit to you that I was wrong, that I shouldn't have left."

"Well, I mean, I did throw a book at your head. So I can't really blame you."

"Yeah. But you missed, at least." They were both werewolves; if Ryn had wanted to hit Kiara in the face with Robin Hobb's *Fool's Fate*, she would have.

"God, we were fuckups." Ryn stroked Kiara's head with her free hand. "I loved you so much I didn't know what to do about it. I just... was so terrified that it was going to change me. I couldn't let you know what I felt. I couldn't allow you that kind of power over me."

"We were kids. We didn't know what we were doing and we didn't know how to do it without hurting each other."

"We're not kids now." Ryn slid her hand down Kiara's cheek and lifted her chin up. She leaned over, and the kiss was soft and sweet and aching. A slow heat infused her bones and rushed hot to the surface of her skin.

Davis groaned, and they pulled apart like two teenagers caught making out at the movies.

Kiara rubbed a hand over her mouth. Her lips still tingled. "Um, maybe let's wait until GNAAW gets here."

Ryn nodded and scooted over so that she sat beside Kiara. Kiara let her head drop to Ryn's shoulder, and Ryn took her hand in both of hers.

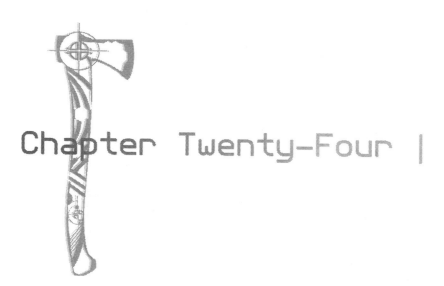

Chapter Twenty-Four |

KIARA RUBBED A HAND OVER her tired eyes. "Did you know there'd be this much paperwork?" she asked Cole.

He looked up from the other side of the kitchen table, where he'd been chewing on the tip of his pen and frowning at the stack of paper in front of him. "I didn't," he said. "I have to do a lot of paperwork at my job, but this is just... ridiculous."

"And why does it all have to be actual paper?" Kiara complained. "I mean, why can't we do it online? Isn't this the age of the Internet?"

"Information. Information Age," Cole corrected while writing something on the form he was working on.

"Whatever. And like, headshots? I don't have a headshot."

"We can take one, or pull it off Facebook, whatever."

"And did you know we have to send a fur sample? For each of us!"

Cole pinched the bridge of his nose. "Yeah, I think I saw that somewhere. I guess it makes sense."

"None of this makes sense," Kiara grumbled.

"Having second thoughts?" He looked up; his eyes showed his concern.

"Maybe. No," Kiara corrected. "Not really. But—I didn't expect that it would be so much work to formalize our pack. I mean, the Huntsmen just needed the symbology." She gestured at her neck.

"The Huntsmen aren't exactly on the same scale as GNAAW. I don't think."

"True," Kiara allowed. There was silence again as they focused on the work. Outside, rain pounded against the windows of their tenth-floor apartment and obscured the view of False Creek and Vancouver's downtown across the water.

Kiara filled out forms, created an outline for the personal essay explaining why, exactly, she wanted to be Alpha of her own pack—she would also need letters from her three supporters explaining their reasons for backing her—and started on another stack of forms.

She and Cole hadn't been lying when they told Ryn that forming a pack was fairly easy—it was—getting the pack formally recognized by GNAAW was the time suck. And even then, it wasn't as though GNAAW didn't already recognize their new pack, but to receive the "full benefits" of the Assembly, they had to do the paperwork.

Kiara was beginning to hate paperwork.

"Do you know Jamie's blood type?" She leaned across the table and tapped her pen against Cole's forearm. He was slumped over the page in front of him and blinked groggily at her.

"No?"

"Seriously?" Kiara shook her head. "You're a paramedic. Shouldn't you know that kind of thing?"

Cole scowled. "I know stuff. I could set your broken leg or deliver your baby. I just... don't know Jamie's blood type." He shifted the focus from himself. "Does GNAAW really need to know that?"

"Apparently." Kiara threw down her pen. "Next thing they're gonna want to know is what six-year-old me wanted to be when I grew up."

"Well, that's easy, and I'm sure they won't judge. I mean, doesn't every little girl dream about being a fighter jet pilot?"

"Shut up." Kiara balled up a scrap of lined paper and threw it at him. "It's not my fault Mom was obsessed with *Top Gun* for like a year."

"You wanted your call sign to be 'Duck-Duck,'" Cole remembered, laughing. "'Cause you thought you and Goose were going to be best friends."

Kiara scrubbed at an imaginary stain on the table. "Mom always made me stop watching before he died. You should have seen how upset I was when I turned thirteen and finally watched the whole thing. I cried for days."

Cole smiled fondly. He reached across the table and took her hand in his. "I'm proud of you, you know. For what you're doing for Ryn, for us."

Kiara flushed, embarrassed. "It's nothing. It's just... paperwork, right?"

"It's not nothing," Cole corrected. "It's something. You're going to be good at this, Kiara. I'm honored to be part of your pack."

Kiara took a deep breath through her nose and ignored the aching lump in her throat. "Quit trying to get out of helping," she said gruffly and shoved another stack at him.

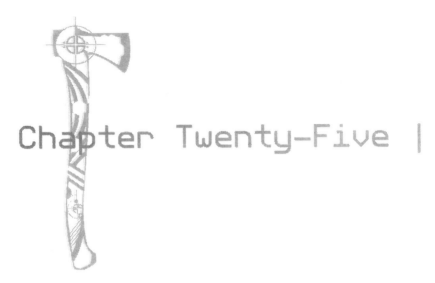

Chapter Twenty-Five |

"ALPHA LYONS."

Kiara nodded in response, ushering the large Black woman into the Olympic Village apartment she shared with Cole. Ryn had been adamant that they not meet with GNAAW in her own space, and Kiara found that reasonable enough.

The new GNAAW rep smiled graciously and stepped inside. Kiara locked the door and followed her into the small living room where Ryn sat.

"You must be Taryn Lee," the rep said. "I'm Renee Anderson, your new rep." She opened the button on her blazer and sat on Kiara's sofa.

Ryn nodded coolly.

Renee smoothed her skirt over her knees and leaned forward with her hands clasped in front of her. "Taryn, I want to formally apologize on behalf of GNAAW. We do, naturally, keep track of all of the lone wolves in North America as best we can. However, that simply involves knowing which city, province, or state they've chosen to live in. We don't want to push ourselves into their lives; we simply need to be aware of any wolves that have the potential to... increase visibility. And, of course, we want to be available should the lone decide they've had enough of their solitude and wish to join a pack. We're a governing body, yes, but we try to guide, not rule."

She pressed her red lips together in not quite a frown. "Mr. Davis should have never leaked the list to the Huntsmen. That's absolutely not what it's for, nor do we believe that a large portion of the lones are a threat to anyone. However, Elliot Brook—"

"Who?" Kiara interrupted.

"Oh, sorry. You probably know him as 'crywolf.'" The woman grimaced. "The... incident with him happened on Mr. Davis' watch, and, as you might be aware, a young woman was killed. Mr. Davis believed that Elliot Brook's lone status contributed to his actions. Davis pushed the matter internally and tried to go through the proper channels to increase surveillance and tracking on lones. We simply don't have the infrastructure for that, nor the desire. Again—" She flashed a sympathetic smile toward Ryn. "We're not trying to infiltrate your lives; we just want to be there for you when you need us."

"Uh-huh." Ryn looked less than convinced.

"When his proposal to the board was turned down, I'm afraid my predecessor took matters into his own hands. We apologize for not being aware sooner of what was happening. We have since discussed this matter with the Huntsmen and told them on no uncertain terms that they are not to act on any names on the list without GNAAW approval."

"I thought their whole thing was that they didn't need GNAAW approval?"

Renee answered Kiara. "Yes, well, times have changed since the stories of the Huntsmen you were probably told as a child. We have a cautious partnership—it's in none of our best interests for our world to overlap too heavily with the humans. In this case, due to Mr. Davis' actions, they did believe they were working *with* us. We've now established a more open line of communication, and believe that will prevent anything like this from happening again."

"They want to cure us." Ryn folded her arms across her chest. "What is GNAAW's position on that?"

"GNAAW officially condemns any form of conversion therapy or treatment."

"And unofficially?"

Renee smiled at them, bland and nonthreatening. "GNAAW acts only in an official capacity."

She wasn't lying—there was no uptick in her pulse, no salty tang of nervous sweat in the air. That didn't mean she was telling the entire truth. Kiara looked at Ryn and was unsure whether she would let it go.

"And what's going to happen to Davis now?" Ryn asked. Kiara swallowed a sigh of relief. Later they could discuss the implications of GNAAW's "partnership." Right now they needed to ensure Ryn's safety.

"I'm afraid I'm unable to share that information with you, but please trust me that he won't be in a position to harm you again."

"Right," Ryn muttered.

"Our privacy and security measures are in place for your protection as well as his," Renee reminded them. "But, shall we move on to more exciting business?" She turned her focus to Kiara.

"On behalf of the General North American Assembly of Werewolves, I'm pleased to formally acknowledge the formation of your pack." Renee reached for her large purse and from the depths pulled out a small metal sculpture.

Kiara had known the twofold purpose for Renee's visit and had anticipated the presentation. What she hadn't anticipated was the way her throat thickened as Renee passed her the sculpture. From her chair, Ryn shot Kiara a concerned look.

Kiara cleared her throat and gently set the sculpture down. "Thank you."

"GNAAW looks forward to building a successful relationship with you, Alpha Lyons. As you come from a GNAAW-registered pack, and have held the title of Alpha-designate in the past, I assume you're relatively familiar with how we work, so I will spare you the info dump." Renee smiled conspiratorially.

She pulled a manila envelope from her cavernous bag and slid it across the table to Kiara. "Inside you'll find your formal identification as a GNAAW-affiliated Alpha, as well as information on how to access our online resources. Additionally, there's a pamphlet outlining our Alpha Development courses, another discussing our volunteer opportunities for you and your pack, as well as an invitation to our AGM later this year if you wish to attend." Renee rose. "It's being held in Seattle this year, so I do hope we'll see you. In the meantime, if you have any questions, here's my business card with my direct line." She handed Kiara the card, a nondescript gray with "Renee Anderson" embossed on the front, "GNAAW" in smaller, discreet letters beneath.

Kiara stood as well. "Thank you," she said.

Renee held out her hand. "I look forward to seeing more of you in the future."

Kiara nodded and shook Renee's hand.

"And Taryn, once again, our apologies. I can assure you, now that this department is under my control—" she flashed a sharp, self-satisfied smile, "—there will be much more oversight to ensure something like this does not happen again." She held out her hand for Ryn, and, after only a moment's hesitation, Ryn rose and shook it.

"Cool," Ryn said. "Good luck."

"Thank you." Renee took her purse and let herself out.

Kiara waited until they could no longer hear the click of Renee's heels in the hallway. "That was... illuminating."

"I like her," Ryn decided. "She doesn't look like she takes any shit."

Kiara hummed in agreement as she reached for the sculpture. It featured four running wolves in the act of leaping over a stream. The wolves were highly detailed, and she ran her fingers lightly over their ridged fur. She turned the sculpture upside down, and traced the engraving on the bottom:

04/06/2017
Kiara Devon Lyons
Cole Stephen Lyons
Jamie Martineau
Taryn Nicole Lee

The lettering was tiny, with plenty of room left to add more names if Kiara's pack grew.

To her complete horror, Kiara burst into tears.

"What? Whoa. Kiara?" Ryn was instantly at her side, dismay written all over her features. "What's wrong?"

Kiara shook her head, unable to speak as sobs wracked her chest. Ryn looked even more alarmed, and pulled Kiara in for a tight hug. Kiara burrowed her face into Ryn's neck. She was grateful for the offered comfort, even though the statue's sharp edges dug into their chests where she still clutched it between them.

"Shh, shh, it's okay; you're okay." Ryn ran a soothing hand down Kiara's back. "I've got you."

"It's just—" Kiara tried between sobs. "My dad—"

"Oh, oh, hon." Ryn squeezed her tighter; her own voice shook. "Your dad always knew you were Alpha material, right? I mean, that's why he made you his heir. He might be mad now, but he'll come around. I'm so sorry." Her voice broke. "This is my fault, not yours, okay? I hate that you're in this position because of me."

"No." Kiara pulled back and scrubbed her face furiously to wipe away the tears. "It's not that." She pulled in a couple deep breaths and had to turn away from Ryn to gather herself.

"I'm going to call him."

"Are you sure?" Ryn reached out a hesitant hand. Kiara took it in hers and gripped tightly.

"Yeah." She wasn't sure how to explain it, but she wanted to hear his voice, even if he was upset.

"Okay." Ryn gave Kiara a kiss on her cheek.

Kiara crossed the room and placed the statue on the mantel of the apartment's small gas fireplace. She adjusted it until it sat perfectly in the middle and ran her fingers over the leaping wolves one last time before stepping back.

She picked up her phone from the table, walked to the balcony, and pulled the sliding door closed. It wasn't raining, but a cool mist hung in the air. She took a breath of it to steady herself and called her dad.

He picked up on the second ring. "Hi, Kiara."

"Hi, Dad." Kiara swallowed around the lump in her throat. "I just… GNAAW just left. It's official now. *We're* official."

There was a long silence. Kiara squeezed her eyes shut against the hot prickle of new tears. God, the last thing she'd ever wanted to do was disappoint her dad, and now—

"You know all those stories I used to tell you about your grandmother?"

That was about the last thing Kiara expected to hear. "Um, yes?"

"About how proud I was of her, that she broke off from her birth pack—they were too conservative and closed-minded, and she wasn't going to be complicit in their bigotry any longer. I told you she was brave, that she'd made a hard choice, but the right one, and that because of her choice we're here now. There are over fifty wolves and humans in the pack your grandmother created."

"I know," Kiara said quietly, too uncertain about where this was going to give in to her rising hope.

"I'll admit I wasn't thrilled when you first told me what you'd done. But I've thought about it a lot since then, and I can't be proud of my mother's choice and not also be proud of yours. I know you didn't come to this decision lightly, and I want you to know that I respect it. You did what was right for your pack, and I'm so proud of you."

"Dad." Kiara's voice broke.

"Your mom and I want you and your pack to know that you'll always be welcomed by ours." Her dad swallowed a chuckle. "Your mom is already demanding to know when you are all going to come for a visit, so I suggest you start planning for that."

"Okay." Kiara fought back more tears. "Yeah. We'll figure out some dates." A loud sniff belied the nonchalance of her words.

"I love you and I'm always going to love you. Even if you aren't in my pack anymore, you're still in my family, and nothing is going to change that." Her dad cleared his throat gruffly. "You make sure you celebrate tonight. This is a beginning, you hear me? Not an ending."

"Got it." Kiara pinched the bridge of her nose with her free hand. She wasn't going to start crying again. She wasn't.

"And say hi to your brother from us."

"Right. Will do."

"Bye, Kiara."

"Love you, Dad."

WHEN SHE CAME INSIDE, MOST of the evidence of her second bout of tears was gone. Kiara found Ryn in the kitchen.

"Was it okay?" Ryn asked nervously.

"Yeah, it was."

Ryn let out the breath she'd been holding. "Good."

"But you were right when you said that I was in this position because of you," Kiara continued. "I wouldn't have left otherwise. I wouldn't have had a good enough reason." She took Ryn's hand in hers. "You've helped me start something amazing. Something that we'll make sure is amazing. Thank you."

Ryn was flustered; her cheeks were pink when Kiara kissed Ryn's knuckles. "You're welcome?"

Kiara drew Ryn closer, kissed away the last of the tension in Ryn's forehead. "We have the chance to make this pack whatever we want. And it started here. With you." She cupped Ryn's face in her hands and looked straight into Ryn's eyes, watching as they darkened when Kiara traced her fingers over Ryn's cheekbones.

"That sounds like a thing we should celebrate," Ryn's voice was a little husky. "Or consummate?" She arched an eyebrow suggestively, but the humor was belied by the unsteady parting of her lips and the heat of her hands as she untucked Kiara's blouse.

Kiara let Ryn pull the blouse over her head and toss it away. She dropped her hands to Ryn's belt and fumbled with the buckle. Her lips sought Ryn's as Ryn steered them toward the bedrooms.

"The one on the left," Kiara advised. Her legs went weak when Ryn grabbed a firm handful of her ass.

Ryn shouldered the door open and kicked it closed. Kiara reached behind her back and unclasped her bra before she wriggled out of her dress pants. Ryn tugged her own T-shirt off and stepped out of her black jeans. She crossed the room and knelt in front of Kiara, who paused in the middle of unclasping her bracelet.

Ryn ran her hands up Kiara's legs, smoothing over the muscles of her calves to slide up Kiara's thighs. Kiara's hands fell to Ryn's shoulders to steady herself when Ryn nosed against the crease of her thigh. Kiara could feel Ryn's breath, hot and damp, through the thin fabric of her panties and, when Ryn gave her a quick nip, Kiara jerked and heat rushed down her limbs.

"What do you want?" Kiara asked breathlessly. She pushed her fingers through Ryn's thick hair; her nails scratched lightly over Ryn's scalp so that Ryn looked up.

"I want to fuck you." Ryn's eyes were steady on Kiara's, arrogant and cocksure. "I want to be inside of you." She slipped a finger under Kiara's panties, then pressed it lightly against Kiara's slick flesh.

Kiara drew in a quick breath; her legs trembled when Ryn worked her finger between Kiara's folds and pushed into her. "I can work with that," she said, to earn a flash of Ryn's grin.

Ryn wrapped a hand more firmly around Kiara's thigh as she added another finger. Kiara was wet enough that they slid in easily, and her eyes fluttered closed as Ryn twisted them to brush against her g-spot.

Ryn kept a steady pace, watching Kiara as her hips jerked and she panted.

Finally, Ryn mouthed at Kiara's clit through the fabric of her panties. The sensation tore through her, and Kiara's hands clenched Ryn's hair as she climaxed.

When the shuddering aftershocks eased, Ryn withdrew her fingers and rose. She led a weak-kneed and breathless Kiara to the bed, making sure she was settled comfortably before she brought her two fingers up to her mouth and sucked them clean. The sight left Kiara's mouth dry.

"Lube?"

"Top drawer." Kiara nodded at the bedside table as she lifted up her hips and wriggled out of her underwear. Ryn crawled across the bed, pulled out the small bottle, and set it on the table before she lay beside Kiara.

Kiara shivered when Ryn's hands ghosted over the hard peaks of her nipples; the touch was so light that it was almost a whisper against her sensitive flesh. She arched up into it. Her own hand rose to pull Ryn down for a kiss that was all heat. Ryn groaned into Kiara's mouth; her delicate touch vanished as she grabbed a fistful of Kiara's breast. Ryn's fingers digging into her sent sparks of lightning through Kiara's body, and her hips pressed beseechingly into Ryn's.

"Please, Ryn," Kiara gasped. Her mouth dropped open when Ryn sucked hard at the nipple she'd been teasing. She could feel Ryn grin against her skin, and Kiara scratched down Ryn's bare back—not enough to break skin, but enough to leave white lines against Ryn's amber skin and have Ryn shudder delightfully against her.

Ryn urged Kiara's legs apart, sliding her hand down between them to cup Kiara's wet heat. Kiara spread her legs wider, thrust herself into Ryn's hand, and moaned at the friction of the heel of Ryn's hand against her clit.

"Can you still come like this?" Ryn asked, a dare in the tilt of her chin. "Just from rubbing yourself against me?"

Kiara's eyes flashed with the challenge. There had always been an element of competition between them, a race and a dare to see who could make the other go boneless first, to see who was too spent to continue. Sometimes the outcome was obvious: when Ryn asked to put as much of herself in Kiara as could fit, or the night Kiara had brought home a sleek bullet vibe for Ryn. But other times that rivalry added a sharp edge to their lovemaking, a gleeful and razor-sharp excitement that had Kiara growing wetter.

Kiara didn't waste time answering Ryn. She moved her hips to press against Ryn's hand, held steady against her. The roll of her clit over that smooth, hard curve of Ryn's hand sent ripples of pleasure through her. Her nipples were rock-hard and ached for attention, and Kiara had to grab a handful of the sheets to stop herself from reaching up to relieve some of that ache—that wasn't part of the challenge, after all.

Ryn bit her lip as Kiara continued to rub against her. Kiara could feel how wet she was, how that wetness slicked against Ryn's skin and made the friction easier. She increased her pace. Her legs trembled as the orgasm built and built until it rolled over her in a crashing wave that bowed Kiara's back off the bed and shoved her clit into Ryn, hard.

"Fuck," Ryn breathed. Her pupils were blown wide; a flush burned her cheeks. She pressed the heel of her hand into Kiara with a sudden, relentless series of quick movements that tore another climax from Kiara and had her crying out soundlessly, unable to draw in enough breath to make a noise.

Before Kiara had fully recovered from the back-to-back orgasms, Ryn slid two fingers into her. She curled them up and rubbed over Kiara's g-spot. Kiara whimpered, half wanting to pull away from the intense sensation, but arching into it. Ryn slowed her movements, thrust her fingers in and out of Kiara with a gentle, soothing rhythm. She took one of Kiara's nipples into her mouth; her tongue flicked against the peak in time with the press of her fingers inside Kiara.

Kiara made a soft noise of disappointment when Ryn's fingers withdrew. Pleasure simmered under the surface of her skin. Ryn rolled her eyes and dropped a quick kiss on Kiara's lips as she reached for the lube. "I'm not done yet, love, don't worry."

Kiara refused to dignify that with a response. Knowing her, Ryn laughed as she flicked open the cap on the lube and slicked her fingers.

The first touch of the cold lube at her ass made Kiara shiver, and Ryn soothed her with an open-mouthed kiss to the jut of Kiara's hip. Ryn's fingers circled gently around Kiara's entrance, her touch so light that Kiara rocked into it, asking for more. At the first slow press of Ryn's finger into her, Kiara bit back a moan. Ryn pressed farther, easing in to the second knuckle. She stilled, allowed Kiara to adjust to the stretch, before she slowly pumped her finger in and out. Kiara closed her eyes as pleasure arrowed up her spine and down her limbs.

When Ryn's movements became easy, Ryn added more lube and gently eased a second finger alongside the first. She worked them into Kiara slowly, inch by inch, until the base of her palm rested against Kiara's cunt. Kiara sucked in a shuddering breath. The sensation of being so filled made her squirm, brushing her labia against Ryn and sending sparks dancing along her skin.

Ryn bent her head between Kiara's legs. She flattened her tongue, laving it over Kiara's clit with rough, hard strokes that made Kiara's toes curl and her breath unsteady. As she pumped both fingers in and out of Kiara's ass, Ryn slid lower and pushed her tongue into Kiara, fucking her in time with the fingers in her ass.

Sweat broke out over Kiara's forehead; her hips lifted off the bed as she arched into Ryn's thrusts. Ryn twisted her fingers, pressed harder with her tongue, and Kiara's entire body clenched and her vision went white as she came with a shuddering sob.

Ryn eased out of Kiara slowly as Kiara came back down to earth. Ryn slid up Kiara's body. Her hands were firm and soothing, pulling her back together when Kiara felt as though all of her had flown apart.

Kiara curled into the touch and clasped Ryn's hands to her chest as Ryn spooned behind her. Ryn's breath was warm on the back of her neck; her skin was hot against Kiara's bare back. Ryn kissed Kiara's shoulder as her breathing finally returned to normal.

Kiara lay there for a minute, five minutes, before she felt able to move. She twisted around so that she and Ryn were face to face.

Ryn smiled and bent forward to nuzzle Kiara's nose. Kiara breathed a laugh and skimmed her hands down Ryn's back.

"Can I taste you?" she asked Ryn as she slid her fingers over the thick band of the boxers Ryn wore.

"Sure." Ryn kissed Kiara, her tongue delving into Kiara's mouth. Kiara could taste herself on Ryn's lips, on her tongue, and she moaned, clutched Ryn's shoulders, and drew her down to the bed.

When they finally broke apart, Kiara gave Ryn's shoulder a gentle shove. "And you know that's not what I meant."

Ryn smiled, lazy and satisfied. "You can. Thanks for asking."

"Of course." Kiara trailed kisses down Ryn's torso, stopping to pull a dusky nipple into her mouth. Ryn's flesh peaked under the attention, and she inhaled sharply when Kiara closed her teeth lightly around the delicate skin.

Kiara moved down from Ryn's nipples. She laved her tongue across Ryn's ribs and dipped into Ryn's belly button just to hear Ryn yelp and push her away. Kiara eased Ryn's underwear down over her hips and kissed each inch of new flesh as it was exposed, until she was able to pull Ryn's underwear off.

Kiara took her time exploring Ryn, nuzzling against the dark thatch of hair between her legs and breathing in the musky scent of her.

Ryn's head fell against Kiara's pillows with a thump when Kiara reached out lightly with the tip of her tongue, brushing it over Ryn's swollen clit. Ryn bucked into the touch, and Kiara complied, flattening her tongue and swirling it over Ryn. Ryn threw a forearm over her mouth to muffle a whimper. Her hips churned as she urged Kiara on. Kiara ran her hands over the undersides of Ryn's legs, spreading them wider so that she could have easier access to Ryn's clit, and sucked it into her mouth.

Ryn tensed beneath her; her body was strung taut. Kiara kept the sucking pressure on Ryn's clit, and added several quick, hard strokes with her tongue over the sensitive nub. Ryn's thighs trembled, and she gave in with a shuddering cry. Kiara continued to lick until Ryn, too sensitive to take it anymore, squirmed and pushed her away.

"Enough," Ryn begged, laughing. "I'm not you—I can't come six times and keep going."

"Mmm, more's the pity."

"One's more than enough for me." Ryn pulled Kiara up beside her and rested her head on Kiara's shoulder.

Kiara stroked Ryn's long hair. It was tangled now, not as terribly as Kiara's, but still a mess. She made a mental note to ask Ryn if she could braid her hair first before they fucked the next time.

"Where's Cole?" Ryn asked, her words a little slurred.

"He went to a movie with Nathan."

"You think he'll be back tonight?"

Kiara shrugged under Ryn's head. "I don't know, why?"

"Because I'm hungry and he cooks. He'd cook for us, right?" Ryn sounded anxious and raised her head.

"Probably." Kiara pressed Ryn's head down. "But I cook now. I can make us something."

Ryn sat up. "You don't cook."

"I can!"

"The last time you tried to cook for me you ruined a pot and the apartment smelled like burned cheese for weeks."

"Well, I can cook now."

Ryn's eyes narrowed.

"I can!" Kiara scowled. "I'll show you."

"Please, don't."

"Oh—" Kiara thought about pushing Ryn off the bed, but settled for just pushing Ryn off her. "Go shower. I'll start prepping dinner."

Ryn looked exceedingly doubtful as she rolled off the bed. "We could get takeout. You don't have to try and—"

"I'm going to make you an eggplant parmesan so good you'll drop down on one knee and propose." Kiara swore.

"What, you believe in marriage now, too?"

"Well, no," Kiara said crossly. "I'll turn down your proposal. But the point is, you'll be so awed by my eggplant parm that you'll make it."

"Right." Ryn hesitated in the doorway. "I mean, that pizza place that Jamie—"

"Go!"

IN THE END, RYN GOT down on one knee, but she didn't propose. Kiara figured that the appreciative, enthusiastic, kitchen oral sex was probably better than a proposal anyway. And she resolved not to let Ryn find out that eggplant parm was the *only* thing she knew how to cook.

Epilogue |

"YOU'VE BEEN USING CHEAP SHAMPOO," Ryn accused. Her eyes were sharp in the mirror and she took an obvious sniff of Kiara's hair. "I could smell that drugstore brand even if I wasn't a werewolf."

Kiara sunk lower into the chair, avoiding Ryn's scolding gaze. "I ran out of the other stuff," she muttered. "Nathan keeps staying over and using it. Which is crap, since he only lives like four blocks—"

"Text me, Kiara! 'Hey, Ryn, love and light of my life, can you please pick me up more shampoo and conditioner when you're at the distributor's?'" Ryn threw up her hands. "It's not like it's hard. Deanna remembers to do it!"

"I do," Deanna agreed. She was sprawled across Ryn's bed with her chin propped up on her elbows as she watched.

Ryn's basement apartment was the second tiniest apartment Kiara had ever seen—Deanna's old place had the dubious honor of being the tiniest. There were two small windows along one side, but as they looked out into the building next door, the apartment didn't get much light. Ryn had made up for that by adding various lamps along the length of it. The apartment was like a long hallway, with a small kitchen at one end and a bed at the other, with the only other door leading to a small bathroom. The lamps added a warm glow to the room, though, and the large painting—an abstract swirl of red—that hung above her bed gave the space a cheerful, lived-in feel. A couple of fake plants added a hint of green, and the chaotic, colorful furniture Ryn had collected somehow all worked together.

"Okay, okay," Kiara surrendered. "I'll text you next time."

"Good." Ryn glared. Kiara fidgeted with the edge of the plastic cape Ryn had draped over her.

Deanna snickered and picked up the wine glass she'd set on the floor. "This is fun. We should do this more often."

"Why are you here again?" Kiara shot back.

Deanna blew her a kiss in the mirror. "Jamie is trying to pack for the trip. I've learned my lesson there—I'm not sticking around to watch the horror show. We went up to Whistler for the weekend last year, and she tore apart the bedroom trying to find her travel toothbrush—which she'd already packed two nights earlier. Watching her freak out is stressful, and then she snaps at you when you try to help." She gestured with her wine glass. "So, I thoughtfully invited myself along."

"So thoughtful," Kiara agreed sarcastically. The robe was itchy around her neck. Ryn bustled around her, fussing with her tools on her tray, and Kiara tried to suppress a shudder.

"If you're going to be a jerk, I won't share my wine," Deanna warned. "This is supposed to be fun. Stop being so jumpy."

"I'm not jumpy," Kiara insisted. And then she yelped and jumped when Ryn sprayed the top of her head with her misting bottle.

"Dude, calm down." Ryn gave Kiara's shoulder a reassuring squeeze. "I've cut your hair before. Why are you acting like I'm going to shave you bald?"

"Nothing. I'm fine." Kiara swallowed and gripped the edges of the chair. "It's just... this AGM is a big thing. I don't want to look silly, or too young, or show up with a rainbow streak."

"Aww," Ryn kissed Kiara's cheek. "That's cute. You'll be fine. And I'm not going to do anything wild, I promise. I'm just going to take about an inch off the ends and clean up your bangs."

"No streak?" Deanna pouted.

Kiara ignored her.

"You know you don't have to go if you're both this nervous," Ryn reminded Kiara. "It's the *annual* general meeting, right? So they'll do one next year."

"I know." Kiara took a couple deep breaths and forced herself to relax as Ryn combed through her hair. "It's our first year as a pack, though. It'd be good to go. And I already took the time off work."

"And Jamie's already probably packed and unpacked her suitcase three times by now," Deanna added. "Plus, I bet they have great swag. Ooh, if there's pins that say 'GNAAW' can you bring me some?"

Kiara rolled her eyes. "I don't think there'll be pins. The whole idea behind GNAAW is to keep the werewolf thing hidden, so I doubt they really want to advertise."

"Oh." Deanna deflated. "Yeah, I guess that makes sense."

"And here I was picturing giant banners like Comic-Con." Ryn flashed Kiara a grin in the mirror as she went to work with the scissors; her movements were quick and efficient.

By the time Ryn had finished, Deanna was happily tipsy and dancing to the Chvrches album she'd found on Ryn's laptop.

Kiara studied her reflection in the mirror. Ryn had been right; Kiara didn't look much different. Her sharp bangs brushed her eyebrows, and the rest of hair fell in a straight line to just past the tops of her shoulders. She reached a tentative hand up and fingered a few strands, admiring the softness.

"Do you like it?"

Kiara flicked her eyes to Ryn, who was standing behind her. She chewed on her bottom lip, and Kiara realized that now it was Ryn who was nervous. Kiara was tempted to make her sweat, but decided not to be cruel.

"I do," she said. "I look like me. But slightly more…" She curled her lip, flashed teeth that could have been fangs. "Badass."

"Cheers to that!" Deanna held up her glass and toasted them. "I never doubted you, Ryn. Not once."

"Thanks." Ryn grabbed Deanna as she danced by and gave her a smacking kiss on the forehead as Deanna squealed in indignation at being lifted off the floor by someone who was practically half her size.

"Quit it," she scolded Ryn, though Kiara didn't miss the pleased flush on her cheeks. Deanna tossed back the last of her wine and picked up her phone. She scrolled through her notifications and let out a groan. "I have a panicked text from Jamie asking where we keep the emergency fire blanket and five missed calls. We'd better get going." She gave Kiara a pointed look, which Kiara took to mean that she was Deanna's ride home.

It was just as well; their flight left in a few hours, and Kiara could pick up Jamie—probably half of Deanna's plan—and get her out of her house so she wouldn't be tempted to upend the place again.

"I'll wait by the car." Deanna winked cheekily. "Give you two a few minutes." She grabbed her purse and sashayed out of the apartment.

Ryn unfastened the plastic cape and shook it out. Kiara stretched, then stepped carefully over the pile of her cut hair on the hardwood floor.

"You'll hold down the fort while I'm gone?"

"I think I can handle the pack, sure." Ryn smirked. "How hard can it be?"

"If you think riding herd on Nathan and Deanna is easy, oh boy, are you in for a rude awakening." Kiara smirked when Ryn paled. "I'm kidding. Everyone's an adult. There's obviously nothing to worry about."

"That doesn't sound like the first line in a horror movie," Ryn said dryly.

"You'll be fine; you're the monster, remember?" Kiara teased.

"Speak for yourself." Ryn slid her hands around Kiara's waist and drew her in for a soft kiss. Kiara melted into it, swaying closer when Ryn deepened it.

"I'm going to miss you," Kiara admitted when they finally pulled apart. She rested her head on Ryn's shoulder, listening to the steady beat of Ryn's heart. They'd only been back together for a few months, but they fit together so seamlessly it seemed longer.

"I'll miss you too." Ryn hugged Kiara tighter. "I know you'll make a good impression."

"I hope so," Kiara said fervently.

Ryn pulled back, forcing Kiara to look up and meet her eyes. "Hey. In the last few months, you faced down the Huntsmen and a vigilante GNAAW rep and formed your own pack. You can handle a bunch of suits, no problem. And I'll be here when you get back."

"You promise?"

"I promise," Ryn said firmly. "You and me, Kiara. You and me. And, obviously, the rest of them, since I guess we're all stuck together now."

"Our own pack." Kiara couldn't resist the glow of pride. "It'll be a good thing to come home to."

"Now get going." Ryn gave Kiara's butt a light slap. "Deanna's waiting."

Kiara stole one last kiss and went out the door.

"ALL GOOD?" DEANNA ASKED FROM where she leaned against the passenger side of the car.

"Yeah," Kiara smiled. "All good."

THE END.

Acknowledgments |

To EVERYONE THIS YEAR WHO has kept me writing, kept me reading, packed and unpacked my kitchen, brought me wine and candles and plants, read first drafts, read second drafts, made sure I ate vegetables, lent me their ears or their backs or their expertise: Thank you. Leita, Claire, Kaschelle, Celeste, Jayne, Kiara, Trever, Scott, Mom, Dad, Wendy, Lisa, Pene, Danica, Hanson, Eliot, Neal, Marcella, Katelyn, Lowell, Chelsey, Jen, Kayla, Devon, Kat, Quinn—you are all incredible and I am so grateful to have you in my life.

Thank you to Interlude Press, to Annie, Candy, Choi, and Nicki, and Zoe, who brought this series to life, and to Monika, for the gorgeous art.

Thank you, RALPH, for Something More.

About the Author |

MICHELLE OSGOOD WRITES QUEER, FEMINIST romance from her tiny apartment in Vancouver, BC. She loves stories in all media, especially those created by Shonda Rhimes, and dreams of one day owning a wine cellar to rival Olivia Pope's. She is active in Vancouver's poly and LGBTQ communities, never turns down a debate about pop culture, and is trying to learn how to cook. Her first novel, *The Better to Kiss You With*, was published by Interlude Press in 2016.

Also by **Michelle Osgood**

The Better to Kiss You With

Deanna, the moderator for Wolf's Run, an online werewolf role-playing game, wanders the local forest with her dog Arthur and daydreams about Jamie, the attractive, enigmatic woman who lives upstairs. When threats from an antagonistic player escalate, Deanna wonders if her job could be riskier than she'd ever imagined—and if her new girlfriend knows more about this community than she had realized.

ISBN (print) 978-1-941530-74-0 | (eBook) 978-1-941530-75-7

You may **also** like...

Storm Season by Pene Henson

When Sydney It-Girl Lien Hong finds herself stranded and alone in the stormy New South Wales outback, her rescue comes in the form of wilderness ranger Claudia Sokolov, whose isolated cabin and soulful singing voice belie a complicated history. While they wait out the weather, the women find an undeniable connection that long outlasts the storm.

ISBN (print) 978-1-945053-16-0 | (eBook) 978-1-945053-29-0

The Seafarer's Kiss by Julia Ember
Published by Duet, an imprint of Interlude Press

After rescuing the maiden Ragna, mermaid Ersel realizes the life she wants is above the sea. But when Ersel's suitor catches them together, she must say goodbye or face brutal justice from the king. Desperate, Ersel makes a deal with Loki and is exiled as a result. To fix her mistakes and be reunited with Ragna, Ersel must outsmart the God of Lies.

ISBN (print) 978-1-945053-20-7 | (eBook) 978-1-945053-34-4

One **story**
can change **everything.**

@interlude**press**

Twitter | Facebook | Instagram | Pinterest | Tumblr

*For a reader's guide to **Huntsmen** and book club prompts,*
please visit interludepress.com.

CPSIA information can be obtained
at www.ICGtesting.com
Printed in the USA
LVOW10s1510090517
533873LV00002B/349/P